Ian Fleming

Illustrated by John Burningham

Chitty Chitty Bang Bang

SCHOLASTIC BOOK SERVICES

NEW YORK • TORONTO • LONDON • AUCKLAND • SYDNEY • TOKYO

ISBN: 0-590-03428-6

Copyright © 1964 by Glidrose Productions Ltd. This edition is
published by Scholastic Book Services, a division of Scholastic
Magazines, Inc., by arrangement with Random House, Inc.

19 18 17 16 15 14 13   01/8

Printed in the U.S.A.

01

Dedication

These stories are affectionately dedicated to the memory of the original CHITTY-CHITTY-BANG-BANG, built in 1920 by Count Zborowski on his estate near Canterbury, England.

She had a pre-1914 war, chain drive, 75 horsepower Mercedes chassis in which was installed a six-cylinder Maybach aero engine — the military type used by the Germans in their Zeppelins.

Four vertical overhead valves per cylinder were operated by exposed push rods and rockers from a camshaft on each side of the crankcase, and two Zenith carburetors were attached, one at each end of a long induction pipe.

She had a gray steel body with an immense polished hood eight feet in length, and weighed over five tons.

In 1921, she won the Hundred M.P.H. Short Handicap at Brooklands at 101 miles per hour, and, in 1922, again at Brooklands, the Lightning Short Handicap. But in that year she was involved in an accident and the Count never raced her again.

I.F.

A Note for the Reader

This story takes place in England and, as in England they use English money — peculiarly enough — the American reader will need to know a little — though not a lot — about English currency. So, a pound is worth approximately $2.80 and a shilling is worth 14 cents. And, if your arithmetic is good enough, you should be able to figure out exactly how much things cost in this story.

Chapter One

MOST MOTORCARS are conglomerations (this is a long word for "bundles") of steel and wire and rubber and plastic, and electricity and oil and gasoline and water, and the toffee papers you pushed down the crack in the back seat last Sunday. Smoke comes out of the back of them and horn-squawks out of the front, and they have white lights like big eyes in front, and red lights behind. And that is about that — just motorcars, tin boxes on wheels for running about in.

But some motorcars — mine, for instance, and perhaps yours — are different. If you get to like them and understand them, if you are kind to them and don't scratch their paint or bang their doors, if you fill them up and pump them up when they need it, if you keep them clean and polished and out of the rain and snow as much as possible, you will find, you MAY find, that they become almost like persons — MORE than just ordinary persons — MAGICAL PERSONS! ! !

You don't believe me? All right then! You just read about this car I'm going to tell you about! I believe you can guess its name already — her name, I should say. And then see if you don't agree with me. *All* motorcars aren't just conglomerations of machinery and fuel. SOME ARE. . . .

Once upon a time there was a family called POTT. There was the father, who had been in the Royal Navy, COMMANDER CARACTACUS POTT. (You may think that Caractacus sounds quite a funny name, but in fact the original Caractacus was the British chieftain who was a sort of Robin Hood in A.D. 48 and led an English army against the Roman invaders. I expect since then there have been plenty of other Caractacuses, but I don't know anything about them.) Then there was the mother, MIMSIE POTT and a pair of eight-year-old twins — JEREMY, who was a black-haired boy, and JEMIMA, who

was a golden-haired girl — and they lived in a wood beside a big lake with an island in the middle. On the other side of the lake, M.20, the big turnpike along the Dover Road, swept away toward the sea. So they had the best of both worlds — lovely woods for catching beetles and finding birds' eggs, with a lake for newts and tadpoles, and a fine big road close by so that they could go off and see the world if they wanted to.

Well, almost, that is. But the truth of the matter was that they hadn't got enough money between them to buy a car. All the money they had went to necessities — food and heat and light and clothes and all those boring things that one doesn't really notice but families have to have. There was only a little left over for birthday and Easter and Christmas presents and occasional surprise outings — the things that REALLY matter.

But the Potts were a happy family who all enjoyed their lives and since they were not in the least sorry for themselves, or sorry that they had no motorcar to go whirling about in, we need not be sorry for them either.

Now Commander Caractacus Pott was an explorer and an inventor and that may have been the reason why the Pott family was not very rich. Exploring places and inventing things can be very exciting indeed, but it is only very seldom that, in your explorations, you discover a really rare butterfly or animal or insect or mineral or plant that people will pay money to see, and practically never that you discover real treasure, like in books — gold bars and diamonds and jewels in an old oak chest.

As for inventions, much the same troubles apply. People all over the world, in America, Russia, China, Japan — let alone

England and Scotland and Wales and Ireland — are inventing or trying to invent things all the time — every kind of thing from rockets that fly to the moon to ways of making India rubber balls bounce higher. Everything, everything, everything is being invented or improved all the time by somebody somewhere — whether by teams of scientists in huge factories and laboratories, or by lonely men sitting and just thinking in tiny workshops without many tools.

Just such a solitary inventor was Commander Caractacus Pott, and I am ashamed to say that, because he was always dreaming of impossible inventions and adventures and explorations in the remotest parts of the earth, he was generally known in the neighborhood as Commander CRACKPOTT! ! You may think it's rude, and so it is, but Commander Pott was a humorous man and he knew his own shortcomings very well, so when he heard that that was his nickname in the neighborhood, he was not at all cross. He just roared with laughter and said, "I'll show 'em!" and disappeared into his workshop and didn't come out for a whole day and a night.

During that time, smoke came out of the

workshop chimney and there were a lot of delicious smells. And when the children put their ears to the locked door, they could hear mysterious bubblings and cooking-poppings, if you know what I mean, but nothing else at all. When Commander Pott came out, he was so hungry that first of all he ate four fried eggs and bacon and drank a huge pot of coffee, and then he asked Mimsie to call Jeremy and Jemima, who were getting in an awful mess digging out a water rat's hole on the bank of the lake. (They never caught the water rat. He dug down faster than they did.)

The twins came and stood side by side looking at their father, wondering what his invention had been this time. (Commander Pott's inventions were sometimes dull things like collapsible coat hangers; sometimes useless things like edible phonograph records; and sometimes clever things that just, only just, wouldn't work, like cubical potatoes [easy to slice and pack and peel but expensive to grow each in its little iron box] and so on.) Commander Pott, looking very mysterious, dug in his pockets and produced a handful of what looked like round colored sugar candies, each a bit bigger than a marble, wrapped in paper. And, still looking mysterious, he chose a red one for Jeremy and a green for Jemima and handed them over.

Well, candies are always candies, thought the children, even though they didn't look very exciting, so they unwrapped them and were just about to pop them in their mouths when Commander Pott cried, "Wait! Look at them first — very, very carefully!"

The children looked at the sweets and Commander Pott said, "What do you see? What's different about them?"

And Jeremy and Jemima said with one voice, or almost, "They've got two small holes drilled through the middle of them."

Commander Pott nodded solemnly. "Now suck them."

So Jeremy and Jemima popped the candies into their mouths and sucked busily away, looking at each other with raised eyebrows as much as to say, "What do you notice? And what do you taste? Mine tastes of strawberry. Mine tastes of peppermint." And both pairs of eyes seemed to say, "They're just candy, round hard candy, and our tongues can feel the holes in them. Otherwise they're just like any other candy."

But Commander Pott, who could easily see what they were thinking, suddenly held up his hand. "Now stop sucking, both of you. Twiddle the candies round with your tongues until they're held between your teeth, with the twin holes pointing outward, open your lips, and BLOW!"

Well, of course the children laughed so much watching each other's faces that they nearly swallowed the candies, but finally, by turning their backs on each other, they managed to compose themselves and fix the candies between their teeth.

And they BLEW!

And do you know what? A wonderful shrill whistle came out, almost like a toy steam engine. The children were so excited that they went on whistling until Commander Pott sternly told them to stop. He held up his hand. "Now go on sucking until I tell you to whistle again." And he took out his watch and carefully observed the minute hand.

"Now!"

This time Jeremy and Jemima didn't laugh so much, but managed to get their candies, which of course were much smaller than before, between their teeth, and they blew like crazy.

This time, because their sucking had hollowed out the holes still more, the whistle was a deep one, like one of the new diesel trains going into a tunnel, and they found that they could play all sorts of tricks, like changing the tone by blocking up one hole with their tongues and half closing their lips so as to make a buzzing whistle, and lots of other variations.

But then, what with their sucking and their blowing, the bit between the two holes collapsed and the candies made one last deep hoot and then crunched, as all candy does in the end, into little bits.

Jeremy and Jemima both jumped up and

down with excitement at Commander Pott's invention and begged for more. Then Commander Pott gave them each a little bag full of the candies and told them to go out into the garden and practice every whistling tune they could think up, as after lunch he was going to take them to SKRUMSHUS LIMITED, the big candy people at their local town, to give a demonstration to Lord Skrumshus who owned the factory.

And as they ran out into the garden, Commander Pott called after them, "They're called 'CRACKPOTS — CRACKPOT WHISTLING SWEETS.' And you know what, my chickabiddies? They're going to buy us a motorcar! !"

But the children were already dancing away into the woods making every kind of whistle you can think of, at the same time sucking like mad at their delicious candies. There really seemed to be something special about Commander Pott's invention — just a little touch of genius.

Well, anyway, I can tell you this, Lord Skrumshus thought so. After he had heard Jeremy and Jemima whistling in his office, he sent them out into the factory and they danced around among the workers, sucking and whistling and handing out candies from their pockets, so that very soon they had all the workers in the factory sucking and whistling, and everyone laughed so much that all the SKRUMSHUS candy machines came to a stop. Lord Skrumshus had to call Jeremy and Jemima away before they brought the whole production of SKRUMSHUS candies and chocolates to a grinding halt.

So Jeremy and Jemima went back into Lord Skrumshus's grand office and there was their father being paid ONE THOUSAND POUNDS by the SKRUMSHUS Company Treassurer, and signing a paper which said he would get an additional ONE SHILLING on every thousand CRACKPOT WHISTLING SWEETS sold by SKRUMSHUS LIMITED. Jeremy and Jemima didn't think that sounded very much, but when I let you into a secret and tell you that SKRUMSHUS LIMITED sells FIVE MILLION every year of just one of their candies called CHOCK-A-HOOP, you can work out for yourself that perhaps, just *perhaps*, COMMANDER CARACTACUS POTT wasn't making such a bad bargain after all.

So then everyone shook hands and Lord Skrumshus gave Jeremy and Jemima each a big free box of samples of all the candies he made. The three of them hurried off back to Mimsie to tell her the good news, and straightaway the whole family hired a taxi and went to the bank to deposit the check for a thousand pounds and then — and THEN they all went off together to BUY A CAR!

Now, I don't know if you got it into your heads yet, but the Pott family wasn't a very conventional family — that is, they were all rather out of the ordinary. Even Mimsie must have been rather an adventurous sort of mother or she wouldn't have married an explorer and inventor like Commander Caractacus Pott, R.N. (Retired) who had, as they say, no visible means of support — meaning he was someone who doesn't do regular work that brings in regular money, but depends on occasional windfalls from lucky explorations or inventions.

So when it came to buying a car, they were all determined that it shouldn't be just ANY car, but something a bit different from everyone else's — not one of those black beetle sedans that looks much the same back and front so that, in the distance, you

22

don't know if it's coming or going, but something rather special — something rather adventurous.

Well, they hunted all that afternoon and all the next day. They looked at brand-new cars and they visited the secondhand showrooms where smart salesmen offered Commander and Mrs. Pott cigarettes and Jeremy and Jemima candies just to try and tempt them to buy. But Commander Pott knew pretty well all there is to know about cars, having been an engineer officer in the Navy and being an inventor as well, and one look under the hood and one trial, listening carefully to the sound of the engine, was generally enough for him — even if he didn't notice that the speedometer had been disconnected or that the chassis was bent because of some crash whose scratches and dents the salesman had carefully painted over. (You have to be very cautious buying ANYTHING secondhand. You never know how careful the last owner has been. And anyway, whatever the thing is, if it is in good order, why does the person want to get rid of it?)

And then at the end of the second day, they came to a broken-down little garage run by a once-famous racing driver. It was really

only a big tin shed with a couple of grimy gas pumps outside, and, inside, the concrete floor was slippery with oil and everywhere there were bits and pieces of old cars that the garage man had been tinkering with, really, as far as one could see, just for the fun of it.

But he was the sort of enthusiast Commander Pott always had a warm corner in his heart for. The two of them went on talking for a long time while Mimsie and Jeremy and Jemima, who were pretty tired by then, grew more and more impatient.

Suddenly they were surprised to see Commander Pott follow the garage man round to the back of his shed where there was a long low object hidden under a tarpaulin. The garage man looked Commander Pott and the family, each one, carefully up and down and then went to one end of the tarpaulin and slowly rolled it back.

Well, I can't tell you how disappointed Mimsie and the children were. From the way the garage man had behaved, they thought there must be some splendid treasure of a car under the tarpaulin. But what did they see? A wreck — that's all. Just the remains, rusty and broken and bent, of a very long, low, four-seater open motorcar without a top and with the green paint peeling off in strips.

"Well, there she is," said the garage man sadly. "She once knew every racing track in Europe. In the old days, there wasn't a famous driver in Britain who hadn't driven her at one time or another. She's still wearing England's racing green, as you can see — that was from early in the thirties.

"She's a twelve-cylinder, eight-liter, supercharged *Paragon Panther*. They only made one of them and then the firm went broke. This is the only one in the world. Doesn't look like much, does she? I'm afraid she's due for the scrap heap. Can't afford to go on giving her living space. They're coming to tow her away next week, as a matter

of fact — take her to the dump, pick her up
in a big grab and drop her between one
of those giant hydraulic presses. One crunch
and it just squashes them into a sort of
square metal biscuit. Then she'll go to a
smelting works to be melted down just for
the raw metal. Seems a shame, doesn't it?
You can almost see from her eyes — those

big Marchal racing headlights — that she
knows what's in store for her. But there it
is. You can see the shape she's in and it
would need hundreds of pounds to get her on
the road again — even supposing there was
someone nowadays who could afford to run
her."

Commander Pott was looking curiously

excited. "Mind if I look her over?"

"Go ahead." The garage man shook his head sadly. "She'd appreciate a last look over by someone like you who knows what real quality used to be."

The whole family picked their way over and through the patches of oily ground. While Commander Pott looked under the hood, Mimsie and Jeremy and Jemima prodded the once-beautiful soft leather upholstery (moths flew out!) ; and looked under the carpets, front and back (beetles scuttled about!) ; and examined the knobs and switches and dials on the dashboard (there were dozens of them, all rusty and mildewed) ; and tried the big old boa-constrictor horn that worked with an India-rubber bulb. But nothing happened except that a

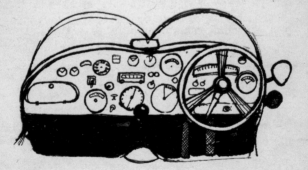

lot of dust blew out of the end into Commander Pott's face as he bent over the engine, peering and tinkering.

The children looked at Mimsie and Mimsie looked back at them and do you know what? They didn't just dolefully shake their heads at each other. They all had the same look in their eyes. The look said, "This must once have been the most beautiful car in the world. If the engine's more or less all right, and if we all set to and scrubbed and painted and mended and polished, do you suppose we could put her back as she used to be? It wouldn't be like having just one of those black beetles that the factories turn out in hundreds and thousands and that all look alike. We'd have a real jewel of a car, something to love and cherish and look after as if it were one of the family!"

Commander Pott took his face out from under the hood. He looked at them and they looked back at him and he just turned to the garage man and said, "I'll buy her. We all love her and we'll make her as good as new. How much do you want for her?"

"Fifty pounds," said the garage man. "She wouldn't fetch much as scrap."

Commander Pott counted out the notes

there and then, and said, "Thank you, and will you please have her towed along to my workshop just as soon as you can."

And do you know? There were almost tears of happiness in the garage man's eyes as he shook them all by the hand. As they climbed into their taxi to go off home, he said seriously, "Commander Pott, Mrs. Pott, Master Pott, and Miss Pott, you will never regret buying that car. She's going to give you the time of your lives. You've saved her from the scrap heap, and I'll eat my hat — if I had a hat to eat — if she doesn't repay you for what you've done today." He was still waving happily after them when they drove out of sight.

As they bowled along in their taxi, Jemima whispered to Jeremy in the front seat next to the driver, "Jeremy, did you notice something very mysterious about the old license plate that was hanging from the back of our car?"

"There was nothing mysterious about it," said Jeremy scornfully, "it was GEN ELEVEN."

"Yes," said Jemima excitedly. "GEN II. Don't you realize what that spells? 'Genii' — like magical people, sort of spirits, like

that story about the Bottle Imp by Robert
Louis Stevenson that Mimsie read to us
once."

"Hum!" said Jeremy thoughtfully.
"Hum! Hum! Hum!" and they sat silently
thinking this odd coincidence over, until
they got home.

Well, the next day Jeremy and Jemima
had to go off to boarding school so they never
saw the arrival of the new car, or rather the
ruins of it, as it came bumping and crashing
down the lane behind the tow truck, but
Mimsie wrote and told them of how it disappeared at once into Commander Pott's
workshop and how their father then locked
himself inside with it and only emerged to
eat and sleep.

For three months, the whole of the summer term, he worked and worked secretly on
the wreck of the old *Paragon* and Mimsie
said that much smoke came out of the chimney and often lights shone all night through

the windows, and mysterious packages arrived from engineering factories all over England and disappeared into the workshop through the locked doors.

Mimsie wrote that their father went through periods of gloom and impatience and frenzy and triumph and dejection and delight and unhappiness and nightmares and loss of appetite, but that gradually, with the passing weeks, he became calmer and happier until, as the holidays came nearer, he was smiling and rubbing his hands. Then at last came the great day when they fetched Jeremy and Jemima from school and the whole family assembled outside the workshop while Commander Pott solemnly unlocked the doors and they all trooped in to where the twelve-cylinder, eight-liter, supercharged *Paragon Panther* stood under the bright lights.

Mimsie and Jeremy and Jemima stood and stared and stared and stared until Jemima broke the silence and said, "But she's the most beautiful car in the world!" Mimsie and Jeremy just nodded their agreement and looked at the *Paragon* with round and shining eyes.

And she *was* beautiful. Every single little

thing had been put right and every detail gleamed and glinted with new paint and polished chrome down to the snarling mouth of the big boa-constrictor horn.

Slowly they walked around her and examined her inch by inch: from the rows and rows of gleaming knobs on the dashboard to the brand-new, dark-red leather upholstery; from the cream-colored collapsible roof to the fine new tires; from the glistening silver of the huge exhaust pipes snaking away from the holes in the bright green hood to the glittering license plates that said GEN II.

And silently they climbed in through the low doors that opened and shut with the most delicious clicks, and Commander Caractacus Pott sat behind the huge steering wheel with Mimsie beside him in her own bucket seat with an armrest, and Jeremy and Jemima got in the back and sank down in the big, soft, red leather cushions and rested their arms on their own armrest between them.

Then, without saying anything, Commander Pott leaned forward and pressed the big black knob of the self-starter.

At first nothing happened. There was just

the soft grinding from the starter motor. Jeremy and Jemima looked at each other with round eyes. Wasn't she going to work after all?

But then Commander Pott pulled out the silver knob of the choke, to feed more gas into the carburetor, and pressed the starter again. And out of the exhaust pipes there came just these four noises — very loudly —

CHITTY-
CHITTY-
BANG-
BANG

And there was a distinct pause between each noise, and it was like two big sneezes and two small explosions. And then there was silence.

Again Jeremy and Jemima looked at each other, now really rather worried. Had something gone wrong?

But Commander Pott just said, "She's a bit cold. Now then!" He pressed the starter again. And this time, after the first two CHITTY sneezes and the two soft BANGS, the BANGS ran on and into each other so as to make a delicious purring rumble such as neither Mimsie nor Jeremy nor Jemima had ever heard before from a piece of machinery. Commander Pott put the big car into gear and slowly they rumbled and roared out of the workshop into the sunshine and up the lane toward the highway, and the springs were soft as silk and always this delicious rumble came out behind from the huge fish-tail exhausts.

When they got to the side road that joined the highway, Commander Pott pressed the big bulb of the boa-constrictor horn and it let out a deep, polite, but rather threatening roar, and then, because he wanted to show everything to the children, Commander Pott pressed the electric horn

button in the middle of the wheel and the klaxon horn fired off a terrific blast of warning:

GA — GOOOO — GA!

Then he steered out on to the highway and they were off on their first practice run.

Well, I can only tell you that the huge, long, gleaming green car almost flew. With a click of the big central gear lever, Commander Pott got out of first gear into second at forty miles per hour, with another click at seventy miles per hour he was in third, and as they touched ONE HUNDRED MILES AN HOUR, he put the huge car into top gear and there they were, passing the black beetle cars almost as if they were standing still.

GA — GOOOO — GA! went the klaxon again and again as they swept down the big, safe, double-lane highway, and the drivers of the little family sedans looked in their rear mirrors and saw the great, gleaming monster whistling toward them and drew to the side to let her go by, and all the drivers said, "COOER! See that! What is she? Smashing! !" And then the green car was past and away and they caught the hurricane howl of the big exhausts and made a note of the number, GEN II, and not one of the drivers noticed what the number really spelled. They just thought it was a nice short number to have and easy to remember.

So CHITTY-CHITTY-BANG-BANG came to the end of the highway and Commander Pott carefully swung the big car into the other lane and roared off back toward home, and Jeremy and Jemima clutched their armrest with excitement and looked over at the glittering dashboard and watched the needle of the speedometer creep back up to a hundred and stay there until they came to the turning off for home. And Commander Pott clamped on the powerful hydraulic brakes until the car was only creeping along and they turned off the highway and bumped back down their narrow lane and back in under the bright lights of the workshop. And, when

Commander Pott switched off the engine, it gave one last CHITTY-CHITTY, let out a deep sigh of contentment, and was silent.

They all climbed out and Commander Pott turned to them with a gleam of triumph in his eye. "Well? What do you think of her?"

And Mimsie said, "Terrific!"

And Jeremy said, "Smashing!"

And Jemima said, "Adorable!"

And Commander Caractacus Pott said mysteriously, "Well, that's good. But I'm warning you. There's something odd about this car. I've put all I know into her, every invention and improvement I could think of, and quite a lot of the thousand pounds we got from the SKRUMSHUS people, but there's more to it than that. She's got some ideas of her own."

"What do you mean?" they all chorused.

"Well," said Commander Pott carefully, "I can't exactly say, but sometimes, in the morning when I came back to get to work again, I'd find that certain modifications, certain changes, had, so to speak, taken place all by themselves during the night, when I wasn't there. Certain — what shall I say? — rather revolutionary and extraordinary adaptations. I can't say more than that, and

I haven't really got to the bottom of it all, but I suspect that this motorcar has thought out, all by herself, certain improvements, certain very extraordinary mechanical devices, just as if she had a mind of her own, just as if she were grateful to us for saving her life, so to speak, and wanted to repay all the loving care we'd given her. And there's another thing. You see all those rows and rows of knobs and buttons and levers and little lights on the dashboard? Well, to tell you the truth, I just haven't been able to discover what they're all for. I know the obvious ones, of course, but there are some of those gadgets that seem to be secret gadgets. We'll find out what they're for in time I suppose, but, for now, I'll admit there are quite a lot of them that have got me really puzzled. She just won't let me find out."

"What do you mean?" asked Jemima excitedly. "Is it a she?"

"Well," said Commander Pott, "that's how I've come to call her. It's funny, but all bits of machinery that people love are made into females. All ships are 'she.' Racing drivers call their cars 'she.' Same thing with airplanes. Don't know about rockets or sputniks — somehow they don't seem very feminine to me — but I bet the rocketeers and sputnicators, or whatever they call the sputnik experts, I bet they call their spaceships and things 'she.' Odd isn't it? I used to serve in a battleship. Gigantic great ship stuffed with guns and radar and so on. Called the *George V*. But we called her 'she.' "

Jeremy said excitedly, "We've got to have a name for her. And I know what we ought to call her. What she called herself."

"What do you mean?"

"What was that?"

"When did she?" they all cried together.

Jeremy said slowly, "She said it when she started — CHITTY-CHITTY, like sneezes, and then BANG-BANG! So we'll call her that, her own invented name."

And the others looked at each other and slowly they all smiled and Commander Caractacus Pott patted the green-and-silver car on her nose and said in a loud and solemn voice, "Now hear me twelve-cylinder, eight-liter, supercharged *Paragon Panther*. We hereby christen you . . ." and they all chorused, "CHITTY-CHITTY-BANG-BANG!" Then they trooped out of the workshop and went happily about all the things they'd forgotten to do for the whole of that exciting afternoon.

The next day was a Saturday and the month was August and the sun positively streamed down. It was a roaster of a day, and at breakfast Commander Pott made an announcement. "Today," he said, "is going to be a roaster, a scorcher. There's only one thing to do, and that's for us to take a delicious picnic and climb into CHITTY-CHITTY-BANG-BANG and dash off down the Dover Road to the sea."

Of course everyone was delighted with the idea and while Commander Pott and Jeremy and Jemima went to get CHITTY-CHITTY-BANG-BANG ready, fill her up with gas, check the water in the radiator, check the oil, test the tire pressures, clean yesterday's squashed flies off the windshield, dust down the body, and polish up the chrome until it shone like silver, Mimsie filled a basket with hard-boiled eggs, cold sausages, bread-and-butter sandwiches, jam puffs (with, of course, like all good jam puffs, more jam than puff), and bottles and bottles of the best fizzy lemonade and orange soda.

Then they all piled into the car, with the top down, of course, and, with CHITTY-CHITTY-BANG-BANG's usual two sneezes and two small explosions, they were off up the lane to the highway that led toward Dover and to the sea some twenty miles away.

But, but, but! And once again, but!!

Twenty-two thousand, six hundred and fifty-four other motorcars full of families (that was the number announced by the Automobile Association the next day) had also decided to drive down the Dover Road to the sea on that beautiful Saturday morning, and there was an endless stream of cars going the same way as the Pott family in CHITTY-CHITTY-BANG-BANG.

Well, Commander Pott drove as cleverly as he could, overtaking when it was safe, weaving like a snake in and out of the traffic, and taking short cuts and side roads to dodge really bad lines of cars. But they made terribly slow progress in spite of much polite mooing of the boa-constrictor horn and, I'm sorry to say, an occasional furious GA-GOOO-GA on the klaxon when some booby in a black beetle insisted on hogging it down the middle of the road and not leaving room for CHITTY-CHITTY-BANG-BANG to get by. As for doing a hundred miles an hour, there just wasn't any question of it, and they crawled along at a miserable twenty. All of them, Commander Pott, Mimsie, Jeremy, and Jemima, were getting more and more hot and impatient, and even CHITTY-CHITTY-BANG-BANG began steaming angrily out of the top of her radiator on which (I'd forgotten to tell you this) there was a silver mascot of a small airplane whose propeller went round and round in the wind, faster or slower according to their speed.

And, although they couldn't see them, CHITTY-CHITTY-BANG-BANG's big head-lamp eyes, that had been so gleaming with happiness and enthusiasm ever since the day before, began to get angrier and angrier and more and more impatient, so that the people who had gazed in admiration at her through the back windows of their cars, became more and more nervous about this gleaming green monster behind them who was beginning to look as if she wanted to eat up, with the silver jaws of her radiator, all the line upon line of black-beetle cars that were getting in her way and keeping her family from their picnic by the sea.

But, all the same, they were making

steady, though very slow, progress, until, outside Canterbury, they came upon a solid jam of cars that must have reached for at least a mile. And there they were — stuck at the back of the line; it really looked as if they couldn't possibly get down to the sands and the sea in time for their picnic — let alone to have a wonderful swim before it.

Suddenly Commander Pott happened to glance at the dashboard, over on the left, opposite Mimsie, and he said excitedly, "I say, all of you, look at that!"

And Mimsie looked and Jeremy and Jemima peered over the back of the seat and among all the knobs and instruments a light on top of a small knob was flashing pale pink! And it was showing a word, and the word said, "PULL!"

"Good heavens!" said Commander Pott. "I wondered what the knob was for, but it's one of the ones I haven't had time to tinker with. What can it be for?"

"Look," cried Mimsie. "The light's turning red!"

And sure enough it was, and now another word was showing! And do you know what the other word said? It said "IDIOT!" So now

the angry red knob read "PULL IDIOT!" And
Commander Pott laughed out loud and said,
"Well I never! That's pretty saucy! Here's
CHITTY-CHITTY-BANG-BANG taking control
and calling me an idiot into the bargain!
Oh, well! Here goes!" And he reached over
and pulled down the little silver lever.

The children, in fact the whole family, sat
on the edge of their seats and waited excitedly to see what would happen.

And a kind of soft humming noise began.
It seemed to come from all over the car —
from the front axle and from the back axle,
and from underneath the hood. And then the
most extraordinary transmogrifications
(which is just a long word for "changes")
began to occur. The big front mudguards
swiveled outward so that they stuck out like
wings sharply swept back, and the smaller
back mudguards did the same (it was lucky
the road was wide, and there was single-lane
traffic, or a neighboring car or a telegraph
pole might have been sliced in half by the
sharp green wings). The wings locked into
position with a click and, at the same time,
though the family couldn't see it from behind, the big radiator grill slid open like a
sliding door, and the big propeller of the fan

belt, together with the flywheel underneath
that runs the gas pump and the electric generator, slowly slid forward until they were
sticking right out in front of the hood of
the car.

And then, on the dashboard, beside another little lever, a *green* light started to
blink and this light said, "PULL DOWN," and
Commander Pott, rather nervously, but this
time obediently, reached over and gingerly
pulled the lever very, very slowly down.

And then, in heaven's name, what do you
think happened?

Yes, you're right, absolutely right. The

wings slowly tilted and, as Commander Pott, at last realizing what CHITTY-CHITTY-BANG-BANG was up to, pressed down the accelerator pedal, the big green car, which was now what I might call an aerocar, tilted up her shining green-and-silver nose and took off! Yes! She took off like an airplane and soared up over the car in front, just missing its roof, and roared away over the long line of stationary cars in the line while all the people stared out of their car windows in absolute astonishment and Commander Pott called out, "Hang on, everyone. For heaven's sake, hang on!" Mimsie and Jeremy and Jemima clutched the armrests beside them and just sat, stiff with excitement and with their eyes and their mouths wide open, thinking, "Heavens above! What is going to happen next?"

Well, what happened next was that there came a shrill whine of machinery and a thump, thump, thump, thump, from under the car and, automatically, the four wheels retracted up into the body so as to be out of the way and let the aerocar go faster without the wind resistance of the wheels to slow her down.

Commander Pott sat gripping the wheel and chuckling with excitement and delight. "I told you so!" he shouted against the roar of the wind. "She's got ideas of her own. She's a magical car. Don't worry! She'll look after us!"

He carefully turned the wheel to see what would happen. And, sure enough, the nose of the car followed what he did and after curving about a bit to get the feel of the steering, Commander Pott made straight for the tall steeple of Canterbury Cathedral in the distance, soaring over the long line of cars in which the poor people were roasting in the sunshine and sniffing up the disgusting gas fumes of the cars in front.

Gradually, as they got confidence, Mimsie and Jeremy and Jemima sat back more comfortably in their seats and Jemima's golden hair streamed out in the wind like a golden flag behind the car and Jeremy's black mop blew about like a golliwog in a hurricane.

Over the solid line of cars they flew — altitude five hundred feet, air speed one hundred miles per hour, engine temperature one hundred and twenty degrees, outside temperature seventy degrees, revolutions of propeller three thousand per minute, visibility five miles — over the river that runs through Canterbury down to the coast, over the houses and over the fields where the cows and the horses and the sheep stampeded about at the roaring noise of this big green dragon they had never seen before, and the shadow of CHITTY-CHITTY-BANG-BANG chased after them over the ground.

Over Canterbury, Commander Pott insisted on circling the tall spire of the Cathedral so that the jackdaws and pigeons flew out of their nooks and crannies squawking and cooing with fright and excitement, and then they headed on over the trees and woods, taking a short cut away from the crowded Dover Road, toward the distant majesty of Dover Castle with its Union Jack flying from the topmost tower.

And, of course, at that speed, in minutes they were over the castle, and again Commander Pott insisted on circling round so that the family (and CHITTY-CHITTY-BANG-BANG for the matter of that) could have a good look, and all the soldiers drilling on the square inside the castle walls look up, much to the rage of their sergeant major, and the sentries too. And between you and me, I think CHITTY-CHITTY-BANG-BANG was lucky to get away without being shot at by the soldiers because, after all, she had no proper aircraft markings, only her GEN II license plates, and, for all the soldiers knew, she might have been some new kind of foreign airplane come to attack the castle, or even a flying bomb, which was really quite what she looked like.

But all went well and they flew on up the coast looking for a place to land to have their picnic beside the sparkling blue sea. But everywhere — St. Margaret's Bay, Walmer, Deal, Sandwich, Ramsgate — all the beaches were crowded with families who had had the same idea as the Pott family, and CHITTY-CHITTY-BANG-BANG's passengers became more and more gloomy as they saw the beautiful sands with their bathers and paddlers and shrimpers, and the rock pools that were certainly crawling with exciting crabs and eels and valuable shells, all crowded with rival holiday makers. And they all longed for a swim and to unpack the bulging picnic basket full of Mimsie's delicious goodies.

Then a curious thing happened. The steering wheel twisted, actually twisted, in Commander Pott's hands as if CHITTY-CHITTY-BANG-BANG realized their disappointment and was taking control herself, and do you know what? CHITTY-CHITTY-BANG-BANG turned away from the coast and soared away over the English Channel *straight out to sea.*

The family held their breath with excitement and Commander Pott wrestled with the wheel and began to look rather nervous. But then the green light started to blink on the dashboard, and now, instead of saying "PULL DOWN" as it had said before, it said "PUSH UP."

And gently Commander Pott pushed up

the little silver lever and gently CHITTY-CHITTY-BANG-BANG began to lose height and plane softly downwards.

"Heavens!" cried Mimsie. "She's going to drop us in the sea! Now we really are in a mess! Get ready to swim, everyone. The cushions will float! Each one hang on to a cushion! The Deal lifeboat will see us and if we keep afloat we'll be all right!"

"Don't worry, Mimsie darling," shouted Commander Pott against the roar of the wind. "It'll be all right. I think I know what CHITTY-CHITTY-BANG-BANG has got in mind. Look there where we're heading for. Those are the Goodwin Sands — acres of beautiful sand that get uncovered during a low tide like this. Why, in summer they even have a football match on the sands. Dover and Deal play each other and get the game over before the tide comes in. Then they row away in boats. And there's the famous South Goodwin Lightship. It's got one of the loudest fog horns in the world and a great revolving light to warn ships away. See the masts of the sunken wrecks sticking up all along the edge of the sands? Probably more ships have been sunk on those sands — from Roman times on — than on any other dangerous rock or reef, or sands, or shoals in the world. All through the ages, it's been a regular graveyard for ships."

"Any chance of finding treasure?" asked Jeremy excitedly.

"I'm afraid there's not a hope," said Commander Pott sadly. "Whenever there's a shipwreck on the Goodwins, particularly on dark or foggy nights, when of course most of the wrecks happen, wreck burglars — they have been known as 'wreckers' since olden times — swarm out from the coast in their sailing boats (they don't use motorboats, so as to be as silent as possible and not warn the men on the lightship who might otherwise radio for a Royal Navy cutter or M.T.B. to come out from Dover and arrest the wreckers and put a guard on board the wreck). These wreckers come slipping softly out and steal everything they can find — they just simply strip the wrecked ship of all its cargo and everything movable and then silently steal away before dawn. So then, when the official salvage craft and tugs put out from Dover in the morning to save what they can and perhaps even try and pull the ship off the sands, they find an empty house, so to speak. The wreckers —

the sea burglars — have stripped her clean as a plucked chicken, and of course, when the police go hunting along the coast for the wreckers, no one knows anything about it and there isn't a sign of the loot because its all been rushed off inland to hideouts by the wreckers' trucks that have been called up secretly. That's how it goes. Just the same as in the bad old days when the wreckers used to shift buoys and warning lights at night to guide ships on to shoals and rocks. That was centuries ago — but the rascals are still at it. Dangerous work of course, putting out from the coast in a sloop or a cutter in a thick fog or a storm, but these wreck burglars are tough, bad men and they're ready to take a chance in exchange for a fat cargo of fine meat and butter from Denmark, or radios and television sets from Germany, or even, sometimes, bars of gold being shipped over to an English bank."

While Commander Pott had been telling these exciting things, CHITTY-CHITTY-BANG-BANG had been planing gently down toward the big expanse of beautiful golden sand lapped by the soft blue ripples of the English Channel and fringed by the masts and the half-sunken hulls of the wrecks that show up at low tide. The crew of the bright, red-painted lightship came up on deck and waved excitedly to them as they soared low overhead and then, as the green light on the dashboard went on winking and Commander Pott gently took his foot off the accelerator, the wheels automatically lowered themselves into position again and they came in to land on the hard, flat, golden surface. The aerocar ran a little way on the sand and then, as Commander Pott put on the brakes, CHITTY-CHITTY-BANG-BANG came to a gentle stop at the edge of the sea. At once, the red light on the dashboard showed again and now it said "PUSH UP" (no "IDIOT" this time).

Commander Pott pushed up the little silver lever and there came the same low hum as the front and back wings slowly folded back to become mudguards again and the big propeller and generator out front slipped back until the two halves of the radiator closed over them. CHITTY-CHITTY-BANG-BANG gave a last two big sneezes and two soft bangs, then Commander Pott switched off the engine, and there was a perfectly good gleaming green car sitting quietly on the huge sandbank in the middle of the sea.

The whole family let out a big "POUFF" of relief and excitement and piled out of the magical car on to the warm sand.

Then, even before they got into their swimming things and began exploring, all the family, of one accord, went up and patted CHITTY-CHITTY-BANG-BANG's warm green hood just as if she'd been alive, and they all said, "Thank you, dear CHITTY-CHITTY-BANG-BANG, you're a real marvel!"

And, do you know, CHITTY-CHITTY-BANG-BANG seemed to let out a long sort of metallic sigh of contentment, which I expect was really only a little steam escaping from the hot radiator, and her big gleaming headlights seemed to dip slightly in modesty and shyness, just as Jemima's eyes do when she's complimented on doing particularly well at her lessons, or her dancing class, or at singing a song, or Jeremy's when he wins a prize for lessons or games.

Then the whole family made a dash to change into their swimming things. And after they had all swum about like dolphins and clambered about among the wrecks, where Jeremy found some quite interesting bits of machinery, and Jemima discovered an old compass that Commander

Pott said he could easily clean up and repair,
they sat down round Mimsie's basket in the
middle of the sands and between them they
ate up every single hard-boiled egg, every
single cold sausage, and every single strawberry jam puff. Then, happy and contented,
they all lay down in the sunshine and,
drowsy and full of good things, and really
quite exhausted with all the excitements of
the day, one by one they dozed off for a little

rest before doing some more swimming and hunting for treasures.

BUT —
BUT —
BUT —

No one noticed that the tide was creeping in over the sands.

No one noticed that the masts of the wrecks were getting lower in the water.

No one heard the glug-glug-glug as the sea quietly, softly flowed into the half-sunken hulls of the wrecked ships.

And no one — not one of the dozing family — noticed that the wheels of CHITTY-CHITTY-BANG-BANG were slowly, inch by inch, being submerged by the incoming tide. And no one realized that soon, very, very soon, the whole family, Commander Pott, Mimsie, Jeremy, and Jemima — and CHITTY-CHITTY-BANG-BANG, who by now was really a member of the family, too — would be marooned out in the middle of the sea — THREATENED WITH MORTAL DANGER! ! !

Chapter Two

To MAKE MATTERS WORSE, one of those summer mists came creeping across the sea, hiding the family and their magical car from the Goodwin Lightship which lies anchored some way to the south of the Goodwins. To warn them and all shipping of the terrible danger of the sands, the lightship began sounding its great foghorn, which is one of the loudest in the world and blinking its dazzling white danger light.

It was CHITTY-CHITTY-BANG-BANG who first woke up to the danger. You see, she had got very hot flying out to the sands and sitting in the sunshine, and as the sea came creeping up, glug-glugging in the hulls of the wrecks and whispering softly over the flat sand, the water gradually submerged the wheels of CHITTY-CHITTY-BANG-BANG. When it reached the bottom of her radiator, she let out a loud warning hiss from the hot metal.

The family opened dozy eyes and then at once they were all on their feet and Commander Pott was running to the car. He jumped in and pressed the self-starter and, with a quick CHITTY! CHITTY! BANG! BANG! of relief, the big car, spinning her wheels in the wet sand so that the spray flew, crept up out of the incoming tide and was steered by Commander Pott up on to the dry center of the rapidly diminishing sandbank where the rest of the family was waiting.

"Quick! Jump in!" he shouted. "We've just got room to take off." But, as Jeremy and Jemima piled into the back seat and Mimsie got in front, already the first little waves had run up the flat sands after them and the bottoms of the tires were awash again.

"My goodness!" said Commander Pott anxiously. "Now we've had it! CHITTY-CHITTY-BANG-BANG can never get up enough speed to take off through the water. The only hope is that the lightship will realize the trouble we're in and send their rescue boat for us. But that'll mean leaving poor CHITTY-CHITTY-BANG-BANG marooned out here alone, and she'll gradually be covered by the sea. During the night, she may easily be washed off the sands into deep water and we'll lose her for ever!"

They all sat there gloomily as the water glugged around them and the fog thickened and there was no sign of a rescue boat. They suddenly realized that they might all be drowned out there in the middle of the English Channel.

All this while, CHITTY-CHITTY-BANG-BANG's engine had been running steadily on, but very soon, any minute now, the level of the sea would be up to her electric generator; there would be the blinding blue flash of a short circuit and the engine would go dead.

Suddenly, amongst the many dials and buttons and levers on the dashboard, a violet light began to blink urgently, showing the words "TURN THE KNOB." And quickly, although Commander Pott didn't know the secret of every one of the row upon row of gadgets on the dashboard, he turned the knob under the violet light, and from underneath the car there came a soft grinding of cogwheels and a curious lifting and shifting of the chassis so that the whole family peered out over the sides to see what was happening.

And do you know what? I bet you can't guess! All four wheels, pointing fore and aft as all car wheels do, had turned and had now flattened out like a hovercraft! Being an inventor, Commander Pott realized what this meant and what the result would be, so he pressed slowly on the accelerator and, just as the waves came up level with the floorboards, all four wheels began to turn like propellers. There was a jerk and CHITTY-CHITTY-BANG-BANG began to move through the water, just like a motorboat, with the four wheels whizzing round and round propelling her forward.

Well, that was all very fine, but she was a heavy car with four people in her and the only way to keep from sinking was to go so fast that they were almost skimming over the surface. So Commander Pott trod the accelerator into the floorboards, there was a great whirl of spray from the four wheels, and CHITTY-CHITTY-BANG-BANG fairly sped across the surface of the sea, kicking up a big bow wave like a speedboat.

Commander Pott had quite a tricky time dodging the masts of the sunken wrecks on the Goodwin Sands, weaving in and out of the tall, rusty iron spikes as if they were involved in some kind of watery maze — but a dangerous one — because if Commander Pott hadn't whirled the wheel this way and that they would have ended up as just another Goodwin wreck. The fog swirled around them, the foghorn from the lightship gave its huge double hoot every two minutes and it really was pretty dangerous and spooky.

To tell the truth, Mimsie and Jeremy and Jemima held their breath and clutched tight to the armrests, expecting any moment to hear a grinding crash and find themselves swimming for dear life. But, somehow, Commander Pott and CHITTY-CHITTY-BANG-BANG between them managed to dodge all the obstacles and soon they were in clear water and swooshing along through the fog.

They had all let out a great "POUFF!" of relief when Jeremy, who had a good sense of direction, said, "But Daddy, aren't we pointing the wrong way? There's the hoot of the

Goodwin Lightship foghorn coming from down on the right. Oughtn't we to sail toward her and then on past her toward Dover?"

Commander Pott said sternly, "You mustn't say 'down to the right.' We're all sailors now. You must say 'to starboard' — that's naval language for 'right.' And at sea 'left' is 'port.' " He twirled the wheel to the left so that CHITTY-CHITTY-BANG-BANG swirled to the left. "Now we're going to port." He turned the wheel to the right. "Now we're going to starboard. Quite easy to remember. 'Port' and 'left' have fewer letters in them than 'right' and 'starboard.' "

"Well, yes," said Jeremy, "that sounds easy. But still, Daddy, whichever way you're going, to port or starboard, I bet you're going the wrong way — away from England, I mean."

At this, Commander Caractacus Pott put on his "secret" face — the face he wore around Christmas time when Jeremy and Jemima asked if they were going to get what they had asked Father Christmas for, and the face he put on when, for instance, he was preparing the Easter egg hunt. All of them, Mimsie and Jeremy and Jemima, recognized their father's "secret" face and waited excitedly for what was to come as CHITTY-CHITTY-BANG-BANG sped on through the fog, throwing up fountains of spray from her whirling wheels, while the sound of the Goodwin Lightship's foghorn got farther and farther away.

"Well," said Commander Pott in his "surprise" voice (he also had a particular voice for springing surprises with), "it's the holidays, isn't it?"

"Yes," they chorused.

"So we'd all like to have a holiday adventure. Right?"

"Yes," they said breathlessly.

"Well," said Commander Pott, "CHITTY-CHITTY-BANG-BANG is going like smoke. The Channel's as flat as a millpond. We've got plenty of gas and the oil pressure's fine, the engine temperature's all right, and the fog will lift the farther we get away from land and it can't be more than about twenty-five miles now to the other side of the Channel and we're doing about thirty knots and a naval knot is 1.15 miles per hour, which gives us a speed of about thirty-five miles per hour, so the whole trip would take less than an hour. And as it's only just five o'clock now," he paused for breath, "and as we've never been abroad, I thought it would be rather fun to GO TO FRANCE!"

"Good heavens!" said Mimsie.

"Gosh!" said Jemima.

"My hat!" said Jeremy.

And, for a moment, they all sat thinking about this colossal adventure. Then Mimsie said, "But we haven't got any passports!"

And Jeremy said, "But don't they have different money in France — francs they're called. What about francs?"

And Jemima said, "What about the language? I've only learned 'oui' which means 'yes,' and 'non' which means 'no.' That's not going to get me very far."

Commander Pott said firmly, "That's no way to treat adventures. Never say 'no' to adventures. Always say 'yes,' otherwise you'll lead a very dull life. Now then, passports — we'll make for Calais, which is dead ahead, and go to the British Consul who represents all English people, from the Queen down, in Calais, and get provisional passports. Money? We've got pounds and we'll change them into francs. Language — Mimsie and I both talk French a bit and if we can't make ourselves understood, we'll find someone who talks English. More people in the world talk English than any other language and we'll soon find someone. Right? Then that's settled. CHITTY-CHITTY-BANG-BANG's going to take us right across the English Channel to France. Now then, we'll turn on the radio and get the weather report for ships and we'll steer a bit more toward the north as there's quite a current running down the Channel and we don't want to be swept along with it and suddenly find ourselves in Portugal or even in Africa." He chuckled. "Do we?"

And all together, and very loud and definitely, they all said, "No, we don't!"

So Commander Pott fiddled with the dials on the radio and out came the familiar voice they had never bothered to listen to before. But now it was very important indeed. It said: "And this is the shipping forecast — North Sea and English Channel: dead calm. Patches of fog near the English coast. Further outlook, unchanged."

Commander Pott switched off the radio. "Well, that's all right. But now we've got to keep our eyes and ears open. The English Channel's always crowded with shipping sailing up and down from London, which is the biggest port in the world, and from Belgium and Holland and Denmark and Sweden and Norway — even from Russia — on its way to and from Africa, India, America, and even as far away as China and Japan. Ships of every nationality use the English Channel and we'd better watch out or we'll be run down."

And, even as he spoke, they heard the giant beat of the engine of a big ship approaching, and Commander Pott quickly sounded the klaxon as a foghorn and it said "GA-GOOO-GA, GA-GOOO-GA," to warn the big ship. Back out of the fog came a series of huge "MOO's," just like the noise a vast iron cow might make, and through the fog, coming straight at them, was the bow of a gigantic white liner.

Well, all I can say is that she missed them by a cat's whisker, and they just had a glimpse of lines of passengers a hundred feet above them, staring down with astonishment at the sight of a green motorcar, using its wheels sideways like propellers, in the middle of the English Channel. Then the huge stern disappeared into the fog leaving them pitching and tossing in the choppy wake.

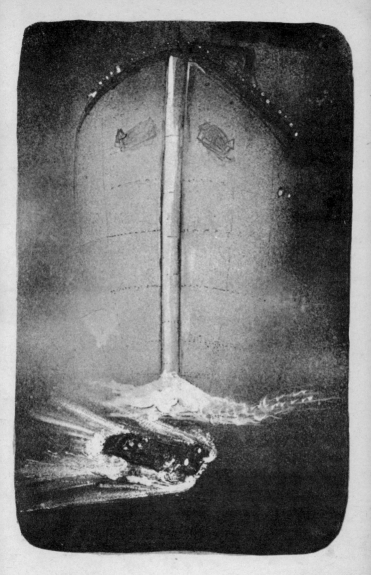

"Whew!" they all said, more or less together. "That was a narrow squeak!" And Commander Pott added, rather unfairly, the others thought, "CHITTY-CHITTY-BANG-BANG, for heaven's sake keep your eyes open and watch where you're going!" This gave him an idea, and he switched the fog lights on and kept on making frequent "GA-GOOO-GA's" on the klaxon.

Well, they heard many more ships passing in both directions, up and down channel, and once the periscope of a submarine came shooting up out of the depths to have a look at them and then quickly slid down underwater again. They imagined word being passed round among the eighty or ninety men of the crew (yes, big submarines carry as many crewmen as that!) "Great Scott! There's a confounded motorcar overhead!"

Then suddenly the fog cleared and they were out in the sunshine with the big white cliffs of France showing up on the horizon and they all let out a cheer that quite surprised the crew of a Dutch SCHUYT (a kind of small barge you see a lot of in the Channel, though, when it's at home, it pronounces itself SKOOT) that happened to be passing. The Dutch crew let out a big HURRAH too, as they gazed in amazement at CHITTY-CHITTY-BANG-BANG whizzing across the calm sea.

They sped happily on, getting nearer to France, and Commander Pott said it was now time to steer north so that they would arrive in the harbor of Calais. But this was easier said than done. The strong current kept drifting them southward and every time Commander Pott turned the wheel to steer north, CHITTY-CHITTY-BANG-BANG had to slow down because her wheels couldn't go round and round like propellers and change direction at the same time. Commander Pott, and in fact all of them, began to get quite worried because there was no doubt that they were going to land on the beach at the base of the gigantic French chalk cliffs that are just as high and steep as the ones

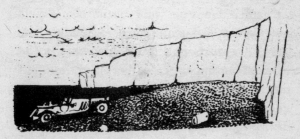

on the English shores near Dover. Sure enough, the water got shallower and shallower until they touched the beach and the violet light on the dashboard blinked urgently and said "TURN THE KNOB." When Commander Pott turned the knob, there came the same purr of machinery under the chassis and the wheels straightened out and clicked back into the straightforward position and they bumped and churned their way up on to the beach.

Of course everyone was very glad to be on dry land again, but nothing could alter the fact that they were stuck at the bottom of giant cliffs that soared up above them toward the sky and the tide was still coming in and it was half past six and there would only be about three more hours of daylight. It really looked as if the whole family, and CHITTY-CHITTY-BANG-BANG, were in the most dreadful and dangerous situation.

Commander Pott said decisively, "Well, it's no good just standing here making long faces. We must split up into two parties and hurry along under the cliffs to right and left and hope that we'll find a little bay somewhere where we can shelter for the night above high water mark. Right? Well now,

Jemima, you come with me along to the left, and Mimsie and Jeremy run off to the right, and let's hope we find a safe place, because otherwise we'll just have to put to sea again and none of us wants to spend the night out in the Channel. All right then, off we go!"

It was Jeremy, running on ahead of Mimsie, who found it. Round a big headland, tucked right in under the cliff so that you couldn't see it from seawards, was the mouth of a CAVE! The sideways opening was quite big, about as big as garage doors, which was the first and most important comparison that came to Jeremy's mind. He called Mimsie and together they went in, over the tide line of seaweed and washed-up cans and bottles and bits of plastic bags and all the other junk that gets carried in on the tide. They could see that, farther in, the cave widened out and got bigger. But then it got a bit spooky and they both decided that the thing to do would be to bring CHITTY-CHITTY-BANG-BANG in with her tremendous lights before they went any farther. So they ran back, scrambling and rattling over the beach, and shouted and called for Commander Pott and Jemima, who presently came back to where Jeremy and Mimsie waited

beside CHITTY-CHITTY-BANG-BANG whose back wheels were already being dangerously approached by the rising tide.

When Commander Pott had heard what they had to say, they all climbed into the car and, with her usual two sneezes and two bangs, she turned and moved slowly, humping and bumping over the beach, toward the cave. At the noise of her great rumbling exhaust, the sea gulls flew screeching out from the top of the cliff and the vibration of her rumble even dislodged small pebbles and scraps of chalk that came tumbling down the gigantic high cliff and once or twice made them cover their heads with their hands and duck.

But they got to the hidden opening to the cave all right, and Commander Pott turned the hood of the car into the opening. They nosed their way in, with a big bump, over the piled-up tide line.

"This is perfect," called Commander Pott. (He had to shout because of the great BOOM-BOOM-BOOM of the exhaust inside the cave.) "It's dry as a bone!" And he switched on the big headlights.

Excitedly, they all peered forward into the cave that seemed to widen out as it burrowed into the cliff until it came to what looked like a corner. "Come on," called Commander Pott. He put CHITTY-CHITTY-BANG-BANG into low gear and they trundled forward over the pebbles while the boom of the exhaust echoed back at them from the walls and the roof just over their heads.

They came to the corner, and round it, and now the cave opened out and became still bigger. There were the marks of pickaxes or chisels of some kind on the walls

that meant that humans had been at work making the cave broader, and there was a straight piece and then another corner and another, and CHITTY-CHITTY-BANG-BANG rumbled and boomed on and Jeremy and Jemima (and their parents too, for the matter of that) were breathless with excitement.

Suddenly Commander Pott called, "Look out!" and there was a great squeaking whoosh, and hundreds and hundreds of bats, disturbed by the noise of the car, swept out over their heads toward the entrance!

But the children weren't particularly frightened by them, because they knew they were
only little harmless mice with wings. They
had often seen them flitting about in the
evening at home. And they knew, too, that
it was all nonsense about bats getting tan-
gled up in your hair (which is an old wives'
tale) because, as Commander Pott had explained to them, bats have the most wonderful built-in radar that works in their heads
with the help of the tips of their big soft
ears, making it almost impossible for them
to collide with anything — as you can see
for yourself by watching them dart about
among the trees in your garden, diving now
and then to catch flies so tiny that the
human eye can hardly see them.

So the children just watched with curios-
ity as the bats poured out over their heads,
and soon their squeaking disappeared and
CHITTY-CHITTY-BANG-BANG came to the *next*
corner. Now they all realized that they were
far from the entrance and deep, deep inside
the cliff, and they wondered, all of them
rather anxiously, what they would find as
CHITTY-CHITTY-BANG-BANG nosed carefully
round the bend between the smooth chalk
walls.

I must admit that what they found was such a shock that even CHITTY-CHITTY-BANG-BANG's exhaust gave a kind of trembly gulp. And Commander Pott himself, who was a very brave man, gave quite a jump in the driving seat and at once put on the brakes and switched off the engine so that there was dead silence in the depths of the cave. As for Mimsie and Jeremy and Jemima, to be quite honest, they went all goose-pimply with fright and just stared and stared at the dreadful thing in front of them — a SKELETON, a human SKELETON, that hung down from the ceiling and swayed softly in the small breeze that blew down the cave!

It was probably only seconds, but it seemed like minutes, that they just sat and stared. And the empty eyeholes in the skull stared back at them and CHITTY-CHITTY-BANG-BANG's big lights showed up each separate bone and the rope that hung down from the roof of the cave and was tied tightly round the skeleton's neck.

Commander Pott spoke first, and it was good to hear his strong, human voice. "This is ridiculous," he said scornfully. "It's nothing but a scarecrow. There are secrets in this cave and someone wants to keep them secret and frighten people away. I vote for going on. What do you all say?"

Mimsie said doubtfully, "If you think it's all right, darling."

And Jemima said, in a rather trembly voice, "After all, it's only a lot of old bones."

And Jeremy said, pretending to forget all about the skeleton, "It would be an awful bore to have to reverse the whole way back again. Besides it'll be jolly exciting to find out the secret of the cave."

And Commander Pott said, "That's the spirit!" (which wasn't a very good choice of words with the ghostly skeleton swaying there in front of them!) "Now we'll just have to push against his knees, so don't be worried by his feet dragging across the car," and he started the engine and moved slowly forward.

Well, as you can imagine, it wasn't very pleasant pushing against the dangling skeleton, feeling its feet scraping over the hood of the car and up over the windshield and flopping down almost into Mimsie's lap and then over the front seat and scraping between Jeremy and Jemima. But they squashed up against the sides of the seats to avoid being touched by the bony toes and, with a last rattle on the trunk, they had left the skeleton behind. Only the silly Jeremy and Jemima *would* look back, and I must admit that they both gave quite a gasp to see the back of the skeleton swaying to and fro and all lit up by the red taillights of CHITTY-CHITTY-BANG-BANG! Then it really did look at its very spookiest, and they quickly swiveled round and gazed firmly ahead.

Now there was no more sand and pebbles on the floor but just beaten down earth and there was quite a slope upward as the cave wound on and on, but you can imagine that the whole family was absolutely agog to discover where the cave led to and what they were going to see round each bend.

Suddenly Commander Pott seemed to listen carefully, and again he stopped the car and switched off the engine. And now they could all hear what he had heard — a frightening, eerie moaning that rose and fell and rose and fell and sent shivers down the spine.

"What's that?" they all asked, trying to keep their voices calm.

Commander Pott leaned forward and un-clipped the spotlight beside the windshield. It was one of the useful spotlights you can use at night as inspection lights and to read high-up road signs. He shone the light care-fully up and along the roof of the cave until the beam came to a sort of contraption strung with shiny copper wires that was fixed into the chalk.

Commander Pott laughed. "That's an old trick," he said cheerfully. "Someone really does want to scare people away from the cave. That's a musical instrument called an aeolian harp. It's much the same as an ordi-nary harp, only the strings or wires are much thinner so that even this small breeze blow-ing along them can make the strings sound this sort of moaning noise. It can get really spooky when the breeze varies and blows hard and soft in turns. I've seen them used before this — in ruined castles in Germany, to give the tourists a fright. Well, it hasn't given these tourists a fright, has it?"

And the others all said, "Oh, no. Rather not," a bit doubtfully — and Commander Pott started up the engine and on they went again, hoping that that was the end of the nasty surprises and wondering all the more who it was who was trying to guard the secret of the cave and what, for the matter of that, the secret could be!

Round the next two bends they crawled carefully along with the thunder of CHITTY-CHITTY-BANG-BANG's exhaust echoing on ahead of them. And then, all of a sudden, on a perfectly straight stretch of cave, CHITTY-CHITTY-BANG-BANG stopped dead!

"Well, that's funny," said Commander Pott, examining the dials in front of him. "We're a bit low on gas, but there's still five gallons. Oil pressure all right, engine temperature a bit high, but not more than it should be going up this sloping tunnel in third gear." And he got out to open the hood and have a look at the engine. He walked round to the front of the car and suddenly stopped. "So that's it!" he said softly. "She saw the trap!"

"What trap?" they all called, leaning out to see.

Commander Pott pointed to a very thin trip-wire stretched knee high from wall to wall across the cave.

He scratched his head and walked up and down the wire, looking at the ground in

front in case there was a trap door to catch
people in, and looking at the walls and the
roof to see if there was some big rock or a
concealed weapon waiting to drop on their
heads as soon as they touched the wire. They
saw him kneel down and examine where the
wire joined the wall and he finally stood up
and said, "Aha! The devils! I've got it!"
Then he walked back to the car and got out a
pair of pliers and some rubber gloves he
always carried for dealing with faults in
CHITTY-CHITTY-BANG-BANG's electrical system.

"What is it?" they asked rather anxiously,
because by now the whole adventure was
getting almost too exciting.

Commander Pott said cheerfully, "Oh,
nothing much. They're only trying to elec-
trocute trespassers and explorers who get
this far into their cave. Probably not actually kill them. Just give them a powerful
shock to frighten them away. But it wouldn't
have been funny if our front bumpers
touched the wire. Might easily have short-
circuited the whole of CHITTY-CHITTY-BANG
BANG's electrical system as well as giving
us all a nasty shock." He looked puzzled.
"Funny the way CHITTY-CHITTY-BANG-BANG

saw the wire and stopped just in time. There really is something almost magical about this car."

(Well, of course, Jeremy and Jemima weren't in the least surprised. They *knew* CHITTY-CHITTY-BANG-BANG was a magical car. Just look at the way she could fly like an airplane and skim across the sea like a speedboat. And anyway, hadn't they had their suspicions on the very first day, when they had noticed that the license plate number GEN II could be read two ways?)

Commander Pott put on his rubber gloves (electricity can't go through rubber) and gave one short snip at the wire and, sure enough, as the pliers cut through, there was a bright blue flash and a shower of sparks and the two halves of the wire fell dead.

And now, when Commander Pott got back into the driving seat and pressed the starter, CHITTY-CHITTY-BANG-BANG's engine at once roared into life again. On they went, climbing still up the wide tunnel of the cave with the big headlights searching ahead for more dangers, and I must say that Jeremy and Jemima in the back seat were quite trembly with excitement at where, in heaven's name, this underground adventure was going to end.

Round the bends they went, on and on into the depths of the chalk cliff, and the speedometer showed that they had now come a whole mile inland from the sea. The air was cold and damp and the breeze, that got stronger and stronger, blew the cobwebs to and fro high up in the roof and made Jeremy and Jemima huddle up together to keep warm.

And then, round a particularly sharp bend, they were suddenly faced with a blank wall of chalk that completely closed the cave. They had come to the end — or at any rate, they seemed to have come to the end — of the long cave!

But Commander Pott got out of the car and walked carefully forward, looking at the ground and the walls and then examining, inch by inch, the chalk wall that blocked the cave. He seemed to find something that excited him very much and he came back to the car and announced, "It's not a wall. It's some kind of a door, a sort of secret trap door. We must find the catch that opens it. Come on, everyone. We must just search every inch of the ground and the walls for it. It'll be something very clever I expect, and well hidden, so tell me if you find even the tiniest clue."

So, inch by inch, the family, working in the bright glare from CHITTY-CHITTY-BANG-BANG'S headlights, began examining what seemed to be a solid wall of chalk blocking the cave — just as if the original cave diggers had decided they couldn't be bothered to burrow any farther. The only clue, which Commander Pott found very early on, was that there was the tiniest crack that wandered, zigzagging, down the middle of the wall. It might have been natural, just a fault in the chalk surface, but again it might not, because through the crack a sharp draft was blowing from the other side.

Jemima had chosen to grub about in the right-hand corner where the wall met the side-wall of the cave. There were a lot of bits of flint embedded in the chalk. (There had been the whole way along the walls and roof of the cave, just like you find in the chalk of any chalk cliff. Some of them are fossils. It's often worth digging them out to see.) Jemima found a jagged piece of flint almost as big as a football. Some instinct made her tug at it and go on tugging

until it suddenly came away in her hand so
that she almost fell over backward. She bent
down and peered into the hole the flint had
left in the chalk and at once she gave a
squawk of excitement and called, "Daddy,
come quickly!" And when Commander Pott
knelt down beside her, he saw what she
had seen — AN ELECTRIC LIGHT SWITCH!

"By golly, you're a clever girl, Jemima! I
do believe you've found the secret." He
called to the other two, "Stand back everyone. I'm going to press down this switch.
Heaven only knows what'll happen. Ready?"
And he pressed down the switch.

From somewhere inside the walls of the
cave, there came a deep rumbling and grinding of machinery as, very slowly, the jagged
zigzag crack in the solid wall widened and
widened and widened until the two halves of
what was really a secret door slid sideways
into deep slots in the side walls of the cave.
And what do you think CHITTY-CHITTY-
BANG-BANG's lights showed through the opening? A huge, vaulted room, quite as big as
the inside of your village church, and all
round the sides were cases and boxes and
barrels and sacks neatly stacked up against
the walls. It was an underground warehouse

— a very secret warehouse for secret things.

What could these things be? And who owned them? And why did the owners want to keep them secret? And why did they want a very private cave leading down through the cliff to the sea? And where were the owners? And, since it all smelled so strongly of secrecy, and therefore probably of unlawfulness, how nasty could these owners be?

These questions and many others ran through all their minds, and Commander Pott put their thoughts in a nutshell when he put his hands on his hips and declared, "Ho hum! I smell dirty work! Now then everyone, switch on the brains! Full power! What do we do next?"

Mimsie, who was, like all mothers, worried about the children, said at once, "Darling, let's close the secret door again and reverse quietly back down the way we came. I don't like the look of this at all."

But Jeremy and Jemima just wouldn't agree to this. They were both the tiniest bit trembly about the way the adventure was going, but they had inherited some of their father's exploring bug and they were terribly eager to discover the secrets of the big underground vault. "Oh, *please*, Mimsie," they both pleaded together, "do let's find out what it's all about."

Commander Pott reflected and said, "Well, Mimsie, after all, no one's going to eat us. And the children don't seem worried. I vote we see the adventure through. It would be ghastly reversing CHITTY-CHITTY-BANG-BANG the whole way back now over a mile of cave to the sea. Besides we've been climbing all the way and we can't be far from the top of the cliff. The cave obviously goes on out of this vault on the other side and leads on to the top. Come on, we'll drive the car up on to the level floor of the vault and give her a rest and then have a good explore. After all, this is pretty thrilling and we really *must* get to the bottom of this secret."

"All right, darling," said Mimsie rather reluctantly. "You know I'm just as keen as you are to find out what this is all about. But if you ask me, there's something pretty fishy about all this — something, well, something criminal. I wouldn't be at all surprised if we hadn't come upon a nest of crooks and gangsters. I only hope none of them appear while we're looking into their secret hoard!"

"Oh, well," said Commander Pott cheerfully, "have to take the rough with the smooth. You never get real adventures without a bit of risk somewhere. Come on!" And they all piled back into CHITTY-CHITTY-BANG-BANG and crept up the last bit of slope until they were parked slap in the middle of the huge secret vault.

While the others piled out and began carefully sniffing about round the edge of the bales and barrels and packages, Commander Pott went back and found the switch on their side of the secret door and, with a grind and a hum of machinery, the two halves came together again. Then he came back and they all systematically began to pry and peer into the secret stocks that were piled up round the walls of the big echoing vault.

Jeremy was the first. "Machine guns," he

cried excitedly, "packed in grease paper. They're in sections ready to be assembled!"

Mimsie said, "Oh, heavens! Boxes and boxes of bombs and hand grenades!"

"Daggers," called Jemima, "all kinds of them. And bayonets with rifles to go with them!"

"Well, I'm dashed," said Commander Pott, "dynamite in these cases, and yards and yards of fuse. And gelignite — the stuff burglars use to blast open safes and vaults."

"Revolvers," called out Jeremy, "automatic pistols. Big ones and small ones — every kind. With boxes and boxes of cartridges."

Mimsie called out anxiously, "Now don't touch anything, children. You can look, but not touch. Something might go off." (Mothers are always thinking something is going to go off — on Guy Fawkes' day, for instance, with the fireworks. And very often mothers are right about this. I must admit that Jeremy and Jemima knew this through one bitter experience with a box of firecrackers, and they were very careful about the way they peered into the boxes and bales.)

So the search went on. And there was no doubt about it, the family had come upon a

great secret arsenal of weapons that certainly hadn't been hidden down in the vault except for some secret and probably criminal purpose.

Finally they all came together again in the middle of the vault and they looked at their father to see what he was going to say about this extraordinary and rather frightening discovery.

Commander Pott had a scruffy bit of paper in his hand and he said, "You know what I think all this stuff is for? In one of the boxes, full of blackjacks and clubs and brass knuckles, there was this scrap of paper that says 'SPECIAL ORDER FOR JOE THE MONSTER, 453 BASHER STREET, SOHO, LONDON.' Now he's the man I've read about from time to time as being responsible for most of the bank robberies and holdups in England that the papers are always full of. But the police have never been able to catch him and they've never even been able to find out where he gets his weapons from. Well, there's no doubt about it. This is his secret arms dump, and I bet my bottom dollar he smuggles what he wants from time to time over the Channel on foggy nights by speedboat. Now," Commander Pott scratched his head, "what do we do next?"

"I know, I know, I know!" cried Jeremy excitedly. "BLOW IT ALL UP!!!"

"Don't be silly, darling," said Mimsie. "What about us and CHITTY-CHITTY-BANG-BANG? Do you want to blow us up too?"

"Well," said Commander Pott thoughtfully, "it would be rather fun, wouldn't it? But first of all we must find the way out of here. The cave must go on to the top of the cliff, or Joe the Monster and his gang couldn't have got all this stuff down here. Now, I've noticed that the draft we've been feeling all the way up the cave is coming from over there." He pointed to the back of the vault. "From behind those huge packing cases. Let's just have a look."

He went over to the packing cases and hauled on the front one and, instead of weighing a ton as they had all expected, it moved easily aside, and so did the next one and the next one. And when he moved the fourth, with the help of the family all tugging and panting, there was the continuation of their cave sloping upwards and, in the distance, there was a pale glimmer of light.

"By golly!" cried Commander Pott.

"That must be the top. Now then, we'll get CHITTY-CHITTY-BANG-BANG through the opening and go on up until we get out of here, and then I'll run back and lay a fuse down the cave to the dynamite and we'll get as far away as possible before the fireworks display." He looked at his watch. "It's after eight, so it'll be dark enough to get the most out of our fireworks. But I'm famished and I know all of you must be, so after the big bang, we'll go off to the nearest town and find somewhere for dinner and bed. We'll certainly all have earned it after this evening's work — if all goes well. And I don't see why it shouldn't."

So they piled back into CHITTY-CHITTY-BANG-BANG and she started up with her two sneezes and two small explosions and they motored between the packing cases and up the slope and out of the secret vault with its huge hoard of explosives and guns that belonged to the biggest crook in England — JOE THE MONSTER!

Outside the vault, Commander Pott stopped the car and went back while the twins watched through the entrance to see what he did. He took a long roll of fuse out of one of the boxes (it looks like stiff thin rope and it's stuffed with magnesium powder or some other quick-burning explosive, rather like the fuse you light when you want to set off a firecracker) and he attached one end to the stacks of dynamite (that comes in oblong sticks) and piled all the gelignite (that's a stiff putty stuff) on top of the dynamite and then he unrolled the length of fuse and came back to the car after blocking up the entrance again with the big crates so that the explosion, when it came, wouldn't chase them up the cave. Then he gave Jeremy the big roll of fuse to unwind as they went along and off went CHITTY-CHITTY-BANG-BANG up the sloping cave toward the distant glimmer of light that was in the entrance.

The entrance was hidden behind a big clump of bushes in an old unused quarry, but CHITTY-CHITTY-BANG-BANG nosed her way through and they bumped and banged across the rough floor of the quarry until they came to a cart track that led away across the fields to one of the French main roads about ten miles away.

It was getting dusky by now, and far away across the fields they could see the side lights of a car that seemed to be coming toward them along the same cart track as they were on. "I expect it's some farmer," said Commander Pott. "Come on, we'd better light the fuse and get away quick or we, and perhaps the farmer too, may get a lump of chalk on our heads. There's a terrific load of explosive down there inside the cave, and heaven knows how much of the cliff we're going to blow up when the fuse gets to the dynamite."

Commander Pott got out of the car, took the rest of the roll of fuse from Jeremy, cut off the end, and threw the rest of the coil into the back of the car. Then he knelt down and put a match to the end of the fuse.

Well, I don't know if you've ever seen a real fuse on fire, but the flame runs almost as fast as *you* can run, and with a tiny bang and a splutter, the little yellow flame darted off across the floor of the quarry back toward the bush which hid the mouth of the cave, and Commander Pott dived for the driver's seat and got CHITTY-CHITTY-BANG-BANG quickly through the gears and racing off along the cart track away from the danger area. When he had gone a good two hundred yards away from the edge of the quarry, he stopped the car and they all looked back and waited, and I must confess that Mimsie and Jeremy and Jemima all had their hands firmly clamped over their ears.

"It must be close now," cried Commander Pott excitedly, and even as he said "now" there came a deep rumbling roar from right down inside the cliff, the ground shook, a great yellow jet of flame shot out of the quarry they had just left, and from the edge of the cliff there came a distant flash and a deep boom, and a pillar of smoke rose slowly into the air as the force of the explosion rushed down the long cave and burst out down by the edge of the sea. Then there came a series of smaller underground explosions and crackles as the ammunition boxes blew up one by one and the bombs and cartridges caught fire, and then there came one last terrific roar and whoosh of flame out of the quarry and to seaward and there was a cracking and rumbling noise in the ground and the cliff top above the cave split open and smoke and flame came out, like a mixture between a volcano and an earthquake. And then the smoking crack in the ground closed again leaving a big dent in the grass where the inside of the cliff had collapsed filling in the underground vault and the remains of the cave.

And then there was silence!

They all let their breath out with a whoosh.

"By golly!!!" (Jemima).

"Gee whiz!!!" (Jeremy).

"Well I never!!!" (Mimsie).

Commander Pott said, "That's the biggest bang I've ever heard. Now come on! We'd better get away quick from here before we have to do any explaining. There's that farmer's car still coming and people will have heard that bang as far away as Calais. They'll even have heard it right across the Channel in England. We'd better steal quietly away and when we get back to England, I'll go and explain things to Scotland Yard.

I bet they won't make a fuss. Probably even give us all medals! It's getting dark, and I bet you're all starving. I know I am." And he put CHITTY-CHITTY-BANG-BANG into gear and she roared along the cart track just as if she was as hungry and thirsty as all of them.

But. But. But!

And again, but!

As they approached what they thought had been a farmer's car, they saw it was a big black open tourer, a very powerful looking car indeed. It had drawn itself right across the track so as not to let them pass, and four men had got out and were standing, or rather crouching down, and they all had revolvers in their hands. One of them, a huge unshaven giant of a man with shoulders as big as a gorilla, came slowly toward where Commander Pott had been forced to pull up. He looked as if he would burst with rage and his eyes were red with fury and his lips were drawn back from his big yellow teeth in a snarl.

Commander Pott whispered, "I regret to have to announce that that's Joe the Monster. I've seen pictures of him outside Police

Stations. And the other three are his gang — Man-Mountain Fink, who's escaped from heaven knows how many prisons — he must be on the run now — Soapy Sam, he's their explosives expert for opening safes ('soap' is the crooks' name for gelignite), and Blood-Money Banks, the blackmailer. Watch out! This is going to be tricky!"

Joe the Monster came up to the car. In his most threatening manner, he growled. "And who might you all be? And what might you all know about that there explosion what's just taken place?"

Commander Pott said innocently. "Explosion? Explosion?" He turned to the children. "Anyone hear an explosion round here?"

Jeremy said brightly, "There was a bit of a pop just now, Daddy. Over by the cliff. You must have missed it."

"Bit of a pop!" Joe the Monster almost exploded himself. He turned round. "Hear that, mates?" He said in a mincing

voice, "They think they may have heard a bit of a pop." He turned back threateningly. "Bit of a pop!!! Call that whopping volcano a bit of a pop? Why it sounded like the end of the world!" Now his voice was an angry growl. "I saw you folks drive up out

of the quarry and I happen, I just happen like, to see a roll of fuse beside those little rascals in the back seat." (Oh dear! thought Jeremy and Jemima together. We ought to have sat on it!) "So do you know what I'm going to do with you and this saucy-looking bus of yours?" He gave a great cackle of cruel laughter. "Why, in exchange for you having blown up my belongings, I'm going to blow up yours and you all with it. See? I'm going to light the end of that fuse and put the lighted end in the gas tank of your fancy motorcar and up you'll all go! How do you like the thought of that, aye, my fine little family of meddlers in other people's business?" He turned to the other gangsters. "Get your guns ready, men, and if any of these rascals try to escape, shoot them down like rabbits. Get it?" The dreadful gangsters cackled with joy at the thought of the sport they were going to have, and the Pott family heard the click of the safety catches going back.

"Now then, you golliwog in the back there, hand over that length of fuse or it'll be the worse for you." And he pointed his revolver straight at Jeremy.

"I won't," said Jeremy stoutly, "and if I'm

a golliwog, you're the ugliest ape outside the London Zoo." And he took the roll of fuse and sat on it.

"Ho-ho!" Joe the Monster grimaced with fury at the insult. "You young whipper-snapper. I'll teach you to do what you're told," and he took a big blackjack out of his pocket and walked purposefully toward the car.

Jeremy had butterflies in his tummy at the sight, but out of the corner of his eye he saw Commander Pott's hand steal across to the little lever that worked the wing mechanism, and, as Joe the Monster drew level with the car, Commander Pott pulled the lever sharply down and CHITTY-CHITTY-BANG-BANG's big green mudguards swung sharply out into their wing-shape. The right-hand wing caught Joe the Monster slap in his tummy and sent him flying head over heels.

"Hang on," shouted Commander Pott. "And keep your heads down." He rammed the accelerator down into the floor boards.

CHITTY-CHITTY-BANG-BANG leaped forward with an angry roar from her twin exhausts and swooped low at the other three gangsters, who just had time to throw them-

selves down on their faces or they would
have been mown down, like Joe the Monster, by the charging wings. And then the
great green aerocar, for that is what she
had become, just cleared the top of the
gangsters' car and roared off toward the
main road.

Of course the gangsters were soon on their

feet and all their guns spat bullets at the
swooping green dragon, but Commander
Pott zigzagged the wheel and, although
there was one bang as a bullet hit the
coachwork, the other bullets whistled harm-
lessly past and the spurting flames of the
revolvers got smaller and smaller in the
dusk.

"Whew!" said Commander Pott. "That was a narrow shave."

The others made whewing noises and thanked heaven for the way their magical CHITTY-CHITTY-BANG-BANG had saved them from the gangsters' terrible revenge.

They got to the main road to Calais and Commander Pott eased CHITTY-CHITTY-BANG-BANG down on to the smooth surface. She gave a bump or two and then was going like the wind down the empty road, with the big head lamps lighting up the way to the distant glow of Calais and the huge feast of omelettes and roast chicken and ice cream they were all looking forward to.

They drew up in front of a nice looking hotel called the "Splendide" (which, as you've guessed, is French for "Splendid") and Commander Pott ordered their rooms and while they tidied up and had a good scrub (much needed by now, as you can guess!), he ordered the delicious dinner in the bright and cheerful dining room and went out to look after CHITTY-CHITTY-BANG-BANG, because, as you know, you must always see that your car is cosy and happy for the night before you look after yourself.

Commander Pott filled up the car with gas and oil and water, checked the batteries and the tires, and drove the car into a comfortable garage beside the hotel. Once he had seen that she seemed contented and in good order, he decided to leave her washing and polishing for the morning, when all the family could help. Then he patted her on her rather hot nose and locked her up for the night and went back into the hotel where the whole family sat down to their delicious dinner before going up to bed for a wonderful and, I'm sure you'll agree, well-earned rest.

BUT! BUT! BUT!

And again, BUT!

Later that night, when they were all fast asleep, a long black car, with Joe the Mon-

ster at the wheel, and Man-Mountain Fink and Soapy Sam and Blood-Money Banks crouching down in the body of the car, came creeping up to the Hotel Splendide in the darkness and hid itself amongst the shadows down a side turning.

Joe the Monster and his gang, still bent on revenge, crept round the ground floor windows of the sleeping hotel looking for a way to break in and get at Commander Pott and his family.

And once again COMMANDER CARACTACUS POTT and MIMSIE and JEREMY and JEMIMA WERE IN MORTAL DANGER!!!

Chapter Three

WHEN JOE THE MONSTER had seen the lights go out in the hotel, and had noticed from the shadows on the blinds that Commander Pott and Mimsie were sleeping in one room with Jeremy and Jemima in another room next door, he and his ruffians got swiftly to work.

From the trunk of the car they took out a number of burglarious instruments — a telescopic aluminum ladder for climbing the walls of the hotel, a jimmy (this is a burglar's tool for opening windows and doors that looks rather like a very powerful can opener), and some rope. Joe the Monster whispered a series of commands and in a trice the gang had run the ladder up the hotel wall to the room where Jeremy and Jemima lay fast asleep. Then, while Man-Mountain Fink, who was as strong and as big as he sounds, held the foot of the ladder, Soapy Sam, who was a very tiny man but a very strong one, crept softly up the ladder and, after some quick work with the jimmy, slipped over the window sill into the room where the twins lay sleeping.

He had had his orders. He went first to Jemima's bed, whirled up the four corners of the sheet on which she was lying, and with her bundled up inside it, tied a knot

out of the four corners so as to make her look like a bundle of washing. And almost before she could awake, he handed her softly out of the window and into the arms of Man-Mountain Fink.

Jeremy had stirred in his sleep, but here again it only needed a few quick movements and he, too, was on his way out of the window. And then their clothes and shoes were hurled pell-mell after them.

But, of course, the children were quickly awake, and even before they could be bundled into the back of the black car, they had started to struggle and squeak.

But, alas, not loud enough!

Mimsie woke up and said sleepily to Commander Pott, "Did you hear that squeaking? It sounded sort of muffled. I suppose it wasn't the children."

But Commander Pott only gave a sleepy grunt and said, "I expect it was bats or mice," and went firmly off to sleep again. And neither of them paid any attention to the sound of the black car starting up and softly driving away.

Fortunately, CHITTY-CHITTY-BANG-BANG had smelled trouble. Heaven knows how, but there it is. There was much about this magical car that even Commander Pott, who was an inventor, a mechanic, and an engineer, couldn't understand. All I can say is that, as the gangsters' low black roadster stole away down the moonlit streets, perhaps its movement jolted something or made some electrical connection in the mysterious insides of CHITTY-CHITTY-BANG-BANG, but anyway, there was the tiny soft whirr of machinery, hardly louder than the buzz of a mosquito, and behind the mascot on the hood a small antenna, like a wireless aerial, rose softly, and the small oval bit of wire mesh in miniature, rather like what you see on top of the big radar towers at airports, began to swivel until it was directly pointing after the gangsters' car which was now hurtling up the great main road toward Paris.

And all through the night, while Commander Pott and Mimsie were asleep, and while the twins were being bumped about in the back of the gangsters' car, CHITTY-CHITTY-BANG-BANG's Radar Eye was following every twist and turn of Joe the Monster, hunched over the wheel of his black tourer.

Now, Joe the Monster was in fact head of

an international gang of robbers and ruffians and he was known in France as Joe le Monstre. (I hope this isn't the first French word you've learned!) And when things got too hot for him in England, he moved his gang over to France and vice versa.

As soon as they got out of the town of Calais, he ordered the knots on top of the sheet bundles which contained Jeremy and Jemima to be undone by Soapy Sam and Blood-Money Banks, between whom the twins were wedged on the back seat. For although he was a monster in the eyes of the law, neither he nor his gang of crooks were so monstrous as to want Jeremy and Jemima to suffocate.

The two children were too startled to know really what was happening to them. They both knew it wasn't something good, but being children of rather adventurous parents, they weren't easily frightened.

Joe the Monster leaned back from the wheel and said over his shoulder, in a voice that was meant to be sugary, "Now then, duckies, everything's quite all right. Your dear pa and ma have asked us to take you for a little night drive to see something of the French countryside by moonlight." He turned to Man-Mountain Fink, who sat beside him, "Ain't that right, Man-Mountain?"

"Absolutely-one-hundred-per-cent-right-and-cross-my-heart-and-wish-to-die," said the big man all in one breath.

"Hear that, my duckies?" called Joe the Monster above the rushing of the wind. "You're in good hands, the very best. You just go off to bye-byes and when you wakey-wakey there'll be a delicious brekky waiting for you."

Now, if there is one thing the twins, and most other children of their age, hate it is being talked to in baby language. Certainly, as far as Jeremy was concerned, he would much prefer Joe to be monstrous rather than niminy-piminy. At least you know where you are with grownups who behave like grownups, but no child likes a grownup to talk like a baby.

But truth to tell, both Jeremy and Jemima were too sleepy from the previous day's adventures to care very much what was happening to them, so they snuggled up together and Jemima was soon fast asleep. But before Jeremy dozed off, he heard snatches of conversation between Joe the

Monster and Man-Mountain Fink drifting back from the front seat.

And the snatches of conversation were something like this: "Just what we want for the Bon-Bon job . . . innocent pair of monkeys . . . shove 'em in just before closing . . . five thousand francs . . . keys of the safe are in the till . . . when the old geyser goes for the change . . . then Soapy can use the jelly."

Trying to make head or tail out of these mysterious sentences, Jeremy snuggled up alongside Jemima and, lulled by the speed of the car and the rush of the wind, and knowing, as children always do know, that their father and mother would soon rescue them, he too went fast asleep.

It had been three o'clock in the morning when the children had been kidnapped from the Hotel Splendide, and it was eight o'clock when the gangsters' car drew up outside a deserted warehouse owned by Joe the Monster in the suburbs of Paris, over 150 miles away from Calais.

And it was precisely at this moment, when the gangsters were carrying the bundled-up children into the building, that the miniature radar on the hood of CHITTY-CHITTY-

BANG-BANG held steady as if she knew that
this was the end of their journey. Then, perhaps because of a short circuit, or perhaps
for some other reason quite beyond my
understanding, CHITTY-CHITTY-BANG-BANG's
powerful klaxon began to go "GA-GOO-GA,
GA-GOO-GA, GA-GOO-GA," and just went on doing it, making the most horrendous din you
can imagine.

Commander Pott and Mimsie were in-
stantly awake, and with, I am sorry to say,
a very powerful swear word (it was "Dash
My Wig and Whiskers," if you want to
know), Commander Pott leaped out of his
bed, pulled on some clothes, and dashed

CARTIER ET FILS

downstairs and round to the garage to find what the electrical fault was and stop it before they had the whole population of Calais, led by the police and the fire brigade, charging round to find out who was responsible for the horrendous din. You can imagine his astonishment when directly he tore open the garage doors and stood face to face with CHITTY-CHITTY-BANG-BANG, there was one last "GOO-GA" and then dead silence.

"Now, what the devil's the matter with you?" said Commander Pott. And as if in reply, the giant head lamps suddenly blazed on and off in one gigantic wink of warning.

Commander Pott was even more puzzled. "There must be something terribly wrong with your electrical system," he said sympathetically. "Let's see what the matter is," and he went to open the hood. But then, for the first time, he caught sight of the thin little radar antenna sticking up in front of the windshield, and he stopped in his tracks. "What in heaven's name . . ." he had just begun, when Mimsie came dashing across from the hotel.

"The children," she cried desperately, "they're gone! And their clothes too! There are the marks of a ladder on the window sill

and somebody's been at the window break-
ing in! They've been kidnapped, I know it,
by those awful men we ran into yesterday!
For heaven's sake, Jack (which she always
used as short for Caractacus), what are we
to do?"

Commander Pott didn't argue, or say are
you sure, or how do you know, or even go to
see the evidence for himself. He knew that
Jeremy and Jemima would never have left
the hotel of their own accord and certainly
not, he added realistically to himself, without having had any breakfast. He looked

from the tearful Mimsie to CHITTY-CHITTY-BANG-BANG and suddenly he knew, he knew absolutely for sure, that that was the meaning of the radar device, and that the magical car had sounded her own horn both to wake them up and because she knew where the twins had gone.

"Here, darling," he said urgently. "Here's some money, be a good girl, and run over and get the rest of my clothes and pay the bill. CHITTY-CHITTY-BANG-BANG knows where they've gone. Don't ask me how, but I know it for sure, and we'll get after them."

As Mimsie ran off, glad to have something

to take her mind away from her fears, Commander Pott jumped into the driving seat and pressed the self-starter, and at once the great car, with her usual:

CHITTY-
CHITTY-
BANG-
BANG

leapt into life and Commander Pott steered her out and across the street just as Mimsie came running out of the hotel.

She jumped in beside him and they were off, slowly at first, so that Commander Pott

could watch the movement of the little radar scanner on the hood just in front of him. At first it pointed left down the main street and then corrected itself just like a compass when it had got on the right course, and then at the big turning toward Paris it swiveled to the right and Commander Pott obediently whirled the wheel and they were off on the huge main road which said "TO PARIS."

Now Commander Pott really trod down hard on the accelerator and the speedometer climbed up and hung around a hundred miles an hour as the great green car, its supercharger screaming like a banshee, positively ate up the kilometers, which, instead of miles, is how they measure distances on the Continent. As each fork or turning in the road came up, he followed the direction indicated by the radar scanner, and with CHITTY-CHITTY-BANG-BANG going lickety-split, lickety-split, lickety-split, they hurtled on toward the gangster hideout where Jeremy and Jemima had been locked into a bare, cell-like room at the back of the deserted warehouse.

Jeremy and Jemima's clothes had been

thrown in with them and they now dressed
quickly and began, in whispers, just in case
anybody might be listening at the door, to
wonder where they were and what was
going to happen to them — and, above all,
when somebody was going to bring their
breakfast.

Jeremy was just telling Jemima about the
mysterious words of Joe the Monster, "doing
the Bon-Bon job" and "Soapy using the
jelly," when the door was unlocked and Joe
the Monster himself came in, beaming (as

far as, with his ugly mug, he could beam),
while behind him Soapy Sam followed with
a tray that he put down on the floor beside
the children (there was no furniture in the
room — not a stick of it).

Jeremy got stoutly to his feet and said, in
as firm a voice as he could muster, "Where
are we and what are you doing with us?
You'll get into bad trouble if you don't take
us back to our parents straight away. You'll
have the police after you any moment now."
And he glared as big a glare as he could
glare into the black-bearded face of the huge
man who towered above him.

"Ha, ha, that's good, that's real good!
Hear that, Soapy? The young 'un says the
cops will be after me." He turned back to
Jeremy and leered hideously down at him.
"Why, my little man, the cops have been
after me since I was smaller than you. Think
of that now, all these years they've been
hunting after me and my pals and they ain't
caught up yet. Often been sniffing at me
heels, mark you, even offered ten thousand
pounds for what they are pleased to call 'information leading to my apprehension,'
which, in English means information on
how to catch me. And now you expect me

to quake in my shoes because of a little English family called POTT! Haw, haw, haw," and he positively shook with demoniac laughter.

Jeremy said angrily, "We're not so little as all that. My father was a Commander in the Navy and he is a famous inventor and explorer, and anyway, besides us, there's CHITTY-CHITTY-BANG-BANG."

"And who might he be?"

"It's not a 'he' it's a 'she' and she's a car, the most wonderful car in the world, she's ma . . ." Jeremy was going to say "magical," but he shut his mouth just in time. Better keep that a secret!

"Oh, you mean that old green rattletrap of yours?" sneered Joe the Monster. "I'll give you that it's certainly a rum old bus — the way it took to the air last evening when we had you cornered. I suppose your inventor Pa has found some way to make a car fly. That right?" Joe the Monster's small piglike eyes became smaller and craftier than ever. "I suppose you've got something there. That invention might be worth a lot of money in the right hands. Now, if you'd like to tell your old pal Joe how it's done, maybe I can take out some patents and give your dad a piece of the money I'd get for sellin' 'em. What about it, young feller, you and me go into partnership sort of?"

Jeremy said bluntly, "I don't know how it works and I wouldn't tell you if I did know."

"Oh well," said Joe the Monster, "I guess I'm not all that keen to go into the motorcar business. Now then, let's get down to brass tacks and then you two youngsters can tuck in to that scrumptious brekky Soapy's brewed up for you. Now then," he looked at them both craftily, "just you both listen to me, and if you do what you're told, you'll come to no harm and even earn yourselves a bit of pocket money into the bargain. And when it's over, I'll see you're both put on a train and sent back to your precious dad and mum in that hotel in Calais."

Jeremy opened his mouth to speak, but Joe the Monster held up a big hairy fist. "Now don't you argue with me, young 'un, and I don't want any more of your lip. Just listen carefully to what you have to do." He paused and spoke slowly, looking from one to the other of them to see that they were paying attention. "Now, all I'm telling you both to do is to go and buy yourselves a big box of chocolates. How would you like that? Just kind of a reward for being such a jolly couple of kids, see? I like kids, I really luv 'em." (Joe the Monster tried to put a sweet, fatherly expression on his face, but all that he could manage was a kind of apelike grimace.) "Now then, not far away from here, twenty minutes' ride, is the most famous chocolate shop in the world. It's called Le Bon-Bon, which, in case you don't know it, is French for candy, and it's run by an old geyser called Monsieur Bon-Bon. He's been in it for fifty years and his dad before him and his grandad before that, and he makes the finest sweets and chocolates in the world, get me? Absolutely the top lollies. Now this here old geyser's a funny old guy and he only opens up his shop for four hours in the middle of the day. Can't be bothered to keep it open any longer because he and his parents have made so much money that he doesn't have to work too hard, see? So he keeps the shop open from ten to twelve in the morning and from two to four in the afternoon. At twelve o'clock this morning, me and my pals are going to drive you round there and give you a pocketful of money and all you've got to do is what I tell you. You walk into the shop and ask for a box of chocolates costing four thousand francs, that's about three English pounds, in the old francs which are the only kind I understand, so you can see it's a fine box of chocolates, eh?" And he looked enquiringly from one to the other.

"Not bad," said Jeremy grudgingly, as if, in his family, they were given a three-pound box of chocolates every day.

"Not bad, he says!" shouted Joe the Monster angrily. "I'll say it's not bad. It's the biggest box of chocolates either of you have ever seen." He quickly calmed down, fished out a pocketbook stuffed with notes and took out one and handed it to Jeremy. "There you are, five thousand francs. I'll tell you what, I'll even let you keep the change. So there you are, duckies, all you do is walk into the shop together when I tell you, hand over the money, and say politely, 'a box of chocolates for four thousand francs, please.' The old geyser don't know much English, but he'll understand that sentence in any language under the sun. Then you hand him that bit of money and take the chocolates and your change, and that's the end of that. Easy job of work, eh? Nice slice of cake. You're a couple of the luckiest kids I ever did see. Now then, you got all that straight?"

They both nodded.

"O.K., then," said Joe the Monster breezily. "Come on, Soapy, and let's get our chow. Looking at the fine breakfast you've dished up for these kids is making me hungry." He turned at the door, "Ta-ta, kiddies, and be good until Uncle Joe comes and fetches you." He walked out followed by Soapy Sam who locked the door behind them.

Well, the china on the old tin tray was pretty chipped and not all that clean. But, by this time, Jeremy and Jemima were ravenous and they cheerfully squatted down on the hard concrete floor and set to.

A French breakfast is very different from an English one. To begin with, French bread, instead of being in loaves, comes in long thin shapes about the length and width of a policeman's billy club, and it's mostly crust, but very delicious crust. The big slab of French butter tasted much more like farm butter than most of the stuff we get in England, and the strawberry jam was very sirupy, like all French jams, but full of big, fat, whole strawberries. The coffee with milk, which the French call "café au lait," was, if you happen to like coffee, better than the wishy-washy stuff you often get in England. So after a bit of rather cautious experimenting, Jeremy and Jemima set to with a will, and in between mouthfuls, cautiously whispered their thoughts and fears about Joe the Monster's plans and, with the help of the snatches of conversation that Jeremy had heard in the car, they came to the following conclusion which, since it's more or less right, I will pass on to you.

They guessed that they were going to be used by Joe the Monster and his gang to rob Monsieur Bon-Bon. They were to be the "innocent pair of monkeys" who would be "shoved in just before closing," while, presumably, the gang waited round the corner with perhaps one of them apparently examining the sweets in the shop window, but really watching the twins through it. Jeremy had been given a five-thousand-franc note to buy a four-thousand-franc box of chocolates, and Monsieur Bon-Bon would have to go to the till to change it. ("Keys of the safe in the till.") As soon as Monsieur Bon-Bon opened the till, the gangsters would dash in and knock him on the head and seize the keys, which were presumably the keys of the

safe where he kept his money.

"But," whispered Jeremy, "I simply can't understand about this business of 'Soapy using the jelly.' What can that mean? There might be jellies in a sweet shop, I suppose. Do you think they are going to gag Monsieur Bon-Bon with his own jellies so that he can't shout for help?"

They both giggled at the idea, but it was Jemima who got the right answer.

"You remember yesterday when we blew up Joe the Monster's stores in that huge cave? Well, Daddy said that some of the cases were full of stuff called gelignite, and he said it was the stuff that gangsters use to blow open safes with. Mightn't 'jelly' be kind of gangster slang for gelignite?"

"You've got it," whispered Jeremy. "By jove, you've got it. That's just what they're going to do. They'll get the keys out of Monsieur Bon-Bon's till and those keys probably open Monsieur Bon-Bon's safe. Now, for heaven's sake, what are we going to do about it?"

At this moment, they heard a key in the lock and Soapy Sam came in to take away the tray and lead them off to wash their hands in an old bathroom at the back of the huge, deserted warehouse. Then they were back in their cell again and the door was locked on them and they squatted together in the farthest corner away from the door and went on with their urgent whispering.

"When we go up to the counter to buy the chocolates," said Jeremy, "we've somehow got to warn Monsieur Bon-Bon that there are gangsters outside, but we don't know half-a-dozen words of French between us. How can we possibly tell him?"

"Could we just make faces and point our fingers at him like guns and shout 'bang'?" said Jemima helpfully.

"He'd think we were just being rude," said Jeremy. "We've got to write him some sort of a note."

"But we haven't got any pens or pencils or even paper."

"We've got the paper," said Jeremy triumphantly, and he produced the big five-thousand-franc note and spread it out between them. "Now if we could just write in big letters 'GANGSTERS' across the note I am sure it's a word Monsieur Bon-Bon will understand. But what can we possibly use for ink?" He looked accusingly at Jemima. "It's a shame you're not a bit older and then you'd have a lipstick. In adventure stories, girls are always using lipsticks to write notes with."

"It's not my fault," whispered Jemima, fiercely. "Anyway I hate the stuff. I once tried Mummy's and I ended up looking as if I'd smeared my face with raspberry jam. Mummy was very angry with me, at least she pretended to be, but I think she was really only trying to stop laughing."

"Well, come on," whispered Jeremy urgently, "it must be getting near the time. I've got absolutely nothing in my pockets except a handkerchief and some bits of string and my pocketknife. What've you got?"

"Nothing, absolutely nothing except my handkerchief," said Jemima despairingly. "But isn't there anything you can do with your knife? It's full of gadgets and things."

"By golly," exclaimed Jeremy, "of course we can use the sharp tip of the corkscrew and punch holes in the bank note to spell out the word 'gangsters' in big letters. Come on, let's get going quickly. You come and sit between me and the door in case anyone looks through the keyhole," and he fished out his pocketknife, opened the corkscrew and set to work with the five-thousand-franc note in front of him on the concrete floor.

They both examined his handiwork and agreed that anyone who handled the note would feel the holes and look at it very suspiciously and almost certainly hold it up to the light to see if the note were so badly damaged that it wasn't worth five thousand francs.

Jeremy had only just stowed the note and his knife away in his pocket when the door opened and Joe the Monster came in followed by Man-Mountain Fink.

"Come on, duckies, time to go," he said jovially. "Now, just one little formality before we set off. I'm sure you kiddies," he looked suspiciously from one to the other, "I'm sure you kiddies haven't been up to any tricks, but, just in case, I'd like to see what's in your pockets."

(Jeremy gave a sigh of relief. Thank heavens they hadn't found a pencil and paper somewhere, or been able to do any of the other tricks they had thought out.)

He innocently emptied his pockets of his pocketknife and handkerchief and showed the five-thousand-franc note, well folded up. Jemima just showed her handkerchief.

After they had been made to pull out the linings of their pockets to show that nothing was hidden, Joe the Monster said, "All right, kiddies, let's go. Remember what you've got to do — you just walk into the shop and ask for a box of chocolates for four thousand francs, right?" And they trooped out, with Man-Mountain Fink taking up the rear to prevent any attempt to escape.

They piled into the black tourer and were soon roaring off through the streets to where,

in the distance, the Eiffel Tower, which is a gigantic tower made of iron right in the middle of Paris, stood up like a huge needle in the sky.

Jeremy kept an eye on the clocks on churches and shops, and he saw that the minutes were hurrying on toward twelve o'clock when, as Joe the Monster had said, Monsieur Bon-Bon closed his shop for the morning. And, sure enough, as they passed a gleaming shop window with the huge

BOX ROW

words "BON-BON" inscribed above it in gold, and turned down the next side street and stopped, Jeremy heard some distant clock begin the first chimes of twelve.

The door of the car was thrown open, and they were hustled out on to the pavement. "Run! Run!" said Joe the Monster, furiously. "We're late and he'll be shutting up his shop. Now don't forget, do exactly what I told you and you'll come to no trouble. If not," and he lifted a big hairy fist as Jeremy and Jemima sped off round the corner.

Sure enough, the doors of Monsieur Bon-Bon's brilliantly lit shop were just closing as they dashed up, and they had no chance to examine the row upon row of delicious candies and chocolates temptingly arrayed in the long window.

A great wave of delicious chocolate smell hit them as they edged in past the closing door, and there was a charming little old man in an old-fashioned suit with an apron round his fat tummy and a long white beard and whiskers, almost like Father Christmas.

He beamed down at the two children and let the door stand open.

"Qu'est-ce que vous désirez?" And from the lift of his eyebrows, the children guessed he was saying, "What do you desire?" Jeremy, panting from the run, managed to stammer out, "A box of chocolates, please, for four thousand francs."

"Aie!" exclaimed Monsieur Bon-Bon, "quatre mille francs — zat ees a very beeg box of chocolates," and he moved over to the counter on which there was an endless array of beautiful boxes tied with huge colored ribbons.

He picked out one, "You like zees one? She is mixed-up chocolates."

Jeremy and Jemima stifled a desire to giggle at his funny English, but it wasn't difficult to stifle the giggle for they knew the danger wasn't over yet and that the terri-

fying part of the adventure was still to come.

"Oh, yes, please," said Jeremy quickly, and, at the same time, over Monsieur Bon-Bon's shoulder, he saw the sly face of Soapy Sam gazing in through the window past all the luscious array of candies and chocolates.

Monsieur Bon-Bon, who was used to the indecision of children and the time they took to make up their minds, looked rather surprised, but he walked behind the counter to wrap up the box and Jeremy followed him and held out with, I admit, a rather trembling hand, the five-thousand-franc note, while Jemima stood beside him biting her knuckles and almost jumping up and down with excitement.

Monsieur Bon-Bon took the note and, as the children had expected, he at once opened it up and felt the holes in it. He looked at them suspiciously, and seeing the urgency and excitement on their faces and somehow smelling a rat, he lifted the note up to the light and softly spelled out the letters one by one. "Gangsters," whispered Jeremy. "Gangsters outside," and he jerked his head toward the door.

Monsieur Bon-Bon was suddenly transformed from a delightful old Father Christmas into a man of action. Without a word, he ran, surprisingly quickly for an old man, across the shop to the door and bolted and barred it, then he pressed down quickly on a big lever beside the door and the steel shutters of the shop rattled down outside, but not before the children had caught a last glimpse of Soapy Sam's face, now contorted into a furious snarl.

Then Monsieur Bon-Bon darted back behind the counter and picked up the telephone, excitedly shouting a lot of French down it amongst which Jeremy and Jemima heard the word "police" used several times. Then Monsieur Bon-Bon put the receiver back on the hook and came round and stood looking down at the children for a minute or two. Then he said, "And now, mes enfants, tell me what zees is all about, yes?"

But as Jeremy began to stammer out his story, from outside in the street came the familiar warning blare of CHITTY-CHITTY-BANG-BANG's tremendous klaxon — "GA-GOO-GA, GA-GOO-GA, GA-GOO-GA," and then a splintering crash of glass and metal and the sound of shouts and people running.

Now, what had happened was this.

CHITTY-CHITTY-BANG-BANG had broken all records in her dash from Calais to Paris, and then, almost seeming to take charge of the steering wheel herself, had finished the trip with a hair-raising sprint through the crowded streets, ignoring traffic lights, police whistles, and the angry shouts of other motorists as if she knew there were only minutes to spare.

Commander Pott clung grimly to the wheel and Mimsie spent most of the time with her hands over her eyes, as if, at any moment, they would crash.

But then the little radar scanner on the hood held steady along one particular stretch of street, and CHITTY-CHITTY-BANG-BANG slowed down all by herself as if she were sniffing about looking for something. And, sure enough, as they passed a big candy shop with the words "BON-BON" in gold upon it, a low black car dashed suddenly out of a side street and Commander Pott and Mimsie just had time to recognize it as the gangsters' car, when CHITTY-CHITTY-BANG-BANG positively wrenched the wheel out of Commander Pott's hands and tore straight, like a charging bull, across the street — straight at the black tourer.

CHITTY-CHITTY-BANG-BANG hit the black tourer bang in its middle with a tremendous crash and tinkling of glass and knocked it right over on its side, spilling Joe the Monster, Soapy Sam, and Man-Mountain Fink out onto the road. And, just at that moment, as the gangsters scrambled to their feet to make a run for it, French motorcycle patrols, with sirens screaming, appeared from both ends of the street and tore down upon them.

Commander Pott jumped from the driver's seat of the now motionless green car, and joined in the chase which now ensued, finally bringing Joe the Monster to the ground with a flying tackle like you see in football.

And then, with the three gangsters lined up and covered with the policemen's revolvers, the door of the candy shop opened and the little man looking rather like Father Christmas came running up followed by Jeremy and Jemima.

Well, you can imagine the scenes of happiness and excitement that followed as the twins were reunited with their parents. But then there had to be a lot of confabulation with the police after a French Black Maria had driven up and taken the shouting and

cursing gangsters away.

But at last everything had been explained in a mixture of English and French, and many compliments were piled on the shy heads of Jeremy and Jemima for the gallant part they had played in bringing about the capture of the gangsters.

Then a police tow truck appeared and hauled the remains of the gangsters' car away and the police promised to have CHITTY-CHITTY-BANG-BANG's broken front bumper and bent-in radiator nose put right as quickly as possible. And Monsieur Bon-Bon and the Pott family watched sympathetically as the great green car was hauled carefully off to a nearby garage, where Commander Pott later visited her to see that she was being properly looked after and that she hadn't suffered any internal damage as a result of her brave ramming of the black tourer.

But she seemed quite happy being attended to by a host of admiring French mechanics, and Commander Pott returned cheerfully to Monsieur Bon-Bon's house over his shop where he had insisted that the whole Pott family should first of all have an enormous lunch and be shown some of the sights of Paris, and then spend the night before going off the next day.

Madame Bon-Bon was just as nice as Monsieur Bon-Bon and there were two rumbustious children about the same age as the twins, called Jacques and Jacqueline, and everyone, talking a mixture of bad French and bad English, got on tremendously well together.

The French police paid several visits during the rest of the day and took everybody's statements in writing, and announced that the Pott family, for their collective efforts in catching the gangsters, would be rewarded no less than one hundred thousand francs, which is about eight hundred pounds, and Madame Bon-Bon added her own reward, which was to reveal the closely guarded secret of the Bon-Bon family on how to make Bon-Bon "Fooj," which was the way she pronounced fudge. (And at the end of this adventure I will pass on to you the recipe, which you will find very easy to make and absolutely delicious.)

The next morning, after another of those wonderful French breakfasts, Commander Pott went round to the garage and, sure

enough, CHITTY-CHITTY-BANG-BANG, although
still wearing a slightly battered look, was
in splendid order and came booming round
to the Bon-Bon shop where the whole Bon-
Bon family insisted on being shown every
detail of her. Then Monsieur Bon-Bon
beckoned Jeremy and Jemima back into
the shop and told them to hold out their
arms, and piled box after box of wonderful
candies and chocolates into them until the
twins could hardly stand upright. And since
the piles of boxes rose higher than their
faces, they could hardly see their way to the
door and had to be helped as they staggered
out to pack their scrumptious presents into

the back of CHITTY-CHITTY-BANG-BANG.

Then there were affectionate farewells all round and both families promised to keep in touch and visit each other whenever they had a chance. (I may say that the families remained firm friends forever after.)

And then CHITTY-CHITTY-BANG-BANG went motoring docilely off down the street with quite a different expression on her face from the furious snarl she had worn in that same street the day before.

They got out onto the open road for Calais and for either the car ferry or the "Air Bridge" to England (they hadn't yet made

up their minds which way to go) and Commander Pott said, over his shoulder, to Jeremy and Jemima, "Well, I think that's quite enough adventure for the time being. It's high time we all went home to peace and quiet."

And Mimsie said, very forcibly, "I entirely agree."

But in the back, Jeremy and Jemima both gave a squawk of protest, "Oh, no," they cried, more or less together. "More adventures! More!"

And at that, believe it or not, there came a whirring of machinery from somewhere deep down inside CHITTY-CHITTY-BANG-BANG. The front and back mudguards swiveled out into the wings, the radiator opened up and the whizzing propeller of the cooling fan slid out and with a tremendous "whoosh" the great green car soared up into the sky.

"My hat," shouted Commander Pott (which was the right thing to shout as his hat had, in fact, been blown off), "I can't control her, she's taken off. Where in heavens is she taking us?"

And, to tell you the truth, even I haven't been let into the secret.

154

TOP SECRET
Monsieur Bon-Bon's Secret "Fooj"

INGREDIENTS:

- 1 lb. granulated sugar
- 1 small can evaporated milk
- ¼ lb. finest butter
- 1 tablespoonful water
- 1 tablespoonful corn sirup
- 4 tablespoonfuls unsweetened chocolate

Put all the ingredients into a saucepan. Melt slowly on a low gas until the mixture thickens slightly and is absolutely smooth. Turn up gas and boil very quickly until it forms into a soft ball when a sample is dropped into cold water. Remove from heat and beat well with a wooden spoon. Pour the whole mixture into a flat, greased pan, mark in squares, and leave to set.

When cold, DEVOUR!

A Note About the Author

Born in England in 1908, and educated at Eton, Sandhurst, the University of Geneva, and the University of Munich, the late Ian Fleming mastered two languages in addition to English — French and German. In 1929, he joined Reuters News Service and was based in London, Berlin, and then Moscow. Following his newspaper work, Mr. Fleming spent two years with a merchant bankers firm and four years with a stock brokerage house. In World War II, he spent a number of years in Intelligence Service, a job which amply qualified him for writing his best-selling spy thrillers about superspy, James Bond.

After the war, Mr. Fleming went back to writing. He became foreign manager for *The Sunday Times* of London, Vice President for Europe of the North American Newspaper Alliance, and foreign manager for the Kemsely Newspapers.